11/14

# The Lubyanka Strategy

## A Novel
## By
## Bob Bonelli

*The Lubyanka Strategy*

A novel by Bob Bonelli

Bob Bonelli (Please visit www.bobbonelli.com)

## Acknowledgement

The author acknowledges the long hours of careful editing by Ruth Ann Bonelli, without whose diligence, support and love this creative endeavor would have been lost.

## About The Author

Bob Bonelli is an accomplished business executive, innovative entrepreneur and writer. Raised in the inner city of Brooklyn, New York, Bob earned a degree in Electrical Engineering and served our nation working for a defense contractor on a classified submarine based missile system. He went on to thirty successful years in the financial industry before returning to his engineering roots and co-founding Adsorbed Natural Gas Products, Inc. in 2011.

Bob has been a guest on Fox News, Fox Business, CNBC, Bloomberg Television and on many Talk Radio programs.

This novel and all of Bob's works are non-stop thrilling page turners, but written with a focus on faith and honor. His stories will touch all of your emotions and challenge your intellect, but without gratuitous scenes or language. Bob Bonelli combines the best of exciting story telling with strong literary style. His works are written to appeal to a wide range of demographics.

# Chapter 1

Oleg felt the cold in the January air as he hurried along the deserted predawn streets of Reutov, a busy city just ten miles east of the center of Moscow. Reutov's active community of residents and commuters will come to life in a few hours but this time of day its streets are abandoned and silent. This morning's quiet was disturbed by the hurried steps of the lone pedestrian. Oleg, a big man whose heavy steps resonate each time his feet hit the cold pavement, saw no other people around him. The rhythmic tapping of the soles of his shoes against the concrete sidewalk quickened as he increased his pace. Each step he takes brings Oleg closer to what he knows is a trap. Decades of experience as a field agent with the former KGB and the current FSB sharpened his senses, and those senses are now screaming for him to go no further. He has no choice. His best friend's life hangs in the balance. Oleg kept moving toward the danger, damning his better judgment.

The call Oleg received on his mobile phone was simple and direct, "The American will be dead in thirty minutes unless you show yourself at Petchetka Street 6-17. Come alone." Oleg had been asleep for just an hour when he was awakened by his phone sounding the arrival of this sinister call. He and his American friend, Tom Moore, were out all night and well into the early morning hours. Tom arrived in Moscow yesterday to celebrate his retirement from the CIA with his old friend and rival. These two friends enjoyed a late dinner and some strong drink. Two veteran agents from different sides of history who share an unbreakable friendship, Oleg and Tom may be past their prime but are still extremely capable of handling any situation.

Has it been thirty-six years since they first met? Was it thirty-one years since Tom saved Oleg's life that night in Berlin? Has it been twenty-five years since Tom joined with Oleg and toasted the birth of Oleg's daughter? All those questions kept repeating in Oleg's thoughts as he approached the location that he is sure will be the place where it all ends. Despite his conclusion on the finality that awaits him, Oleg knows that he is Tom's only chance for survival and he continued forward.

Oleg reached into the right pocket of his heavy dress coat to feel the reassurance of his semi-automatic MP-443 Grach pistol. The weapon was charged with one round in the chamber and sixteen rounds remaining in its magazine. Two additional fully loaded seventeen round magazines in the other pocket of his coat and the rounds in the gun will have to be enough. There was no time to prepare further. He quickened his pace as he looked at his watch and realized he had little time left to cover the remaining distance to the address specified by the caller.

It took Oleg another ten minutes to arrive at the intersection of Petchetka Street and Herzen Boulevard. He hurried down Petchetka Street to number 6-17, a six story Soviet era building. The main entrance to the building is a long enough distance from the Boulevard to be shielded from the bright street lamps lighting the intersection against the blackness of the early morning.

Oleg instinctively stopped as he approached the darkened entrance and assessed the conditions. The lobby was also dark. A narrow alley, covered with three feet of undisturbed snow that fell only two days ago, separated the building from the one next to it. Oleg observed there were no footprints. He looked up, taking advantage of the clear dark sky, and saw no obvious movement on the edge of the roof line. He knew he was being watched but it didn't matter. He had no time to enter undetected so he would have to rely on his experience and reflexes. Understanding the time was at hand, Oleg walked through the unlocked entrance and into the blacked out lobby.

"This way," said a voice from the darkness, as the lobby lights slowly came to life. The fresh light contrasted with the prior darkness and made Oleg's eyes squint. His sight quickly adjusted and he saw three men dressed in boots, dark pants and heavy waist length jackets. The men had full facial ski masks with small openings for their eyes, and each man was armed with an AK-47 assault rifle. The rifles were all pointed directly at Oleg. Two of the men stepped behind Oleg and the third remained in front and led the way. They did not stop to search him because the barrels of two weapons were only inches from Oleg's head. The four walked from the lobby, down a short hallway and through the door of a first floor office suite.

As soon as they entered the suite Oleg saw Tom, who sat bound to a chair with his hands behind him. The chair was in the middle of an open area surrounded by plain half wall cubicles. Three more men dressed and armed exactly as the three from the lobby, were standing between Tom and Oleg. This group's rifles were aimed at Tom. A seventh man stood up from behind the cubicle to the right of where Tom was sitting. The man, wearing an expensive dress coat opened to reveal a well-tailored business suit, starred at Oleg and asked, "The key. Where is the key?"

Oleg looked at Tom to see that his friend clearly did not end up in the chair willingly. The bruises on Tom's face told the story of his resistance. The short and thinly built American had clearly suffered a beating, but Tom's small stature masked his incredible toughness and remarkable endurance. Oleg starred at his friend, saw that familiar look in his eye and knew his old friend was ready and still had plenty of fight left in him.

The man in the suit took out a Grach from his coat pocket and walked slowly over to Tom. Reaching the chair, the man pulled back the slide and charged the weapon. He put the front of the barrel directly against

Tom's right temple. "I will shoot him in two seconds unless you tell me where I can find the key and I will not give you three," the man said.

Tom looked directly at Oleg and winked his left eye. That was the go signal. Tom, who had managed to free himself, stood up grabbing the Grach and fired a single shot into the head of the man in the suit. As soon as Tom winked Oleg pulled his charged MP-443 turned and fired three successive rounds, one each hitting between the eye slits of the ski masks of the three stunned thugs guarding him. They all fell dead. Simultaneously, Tom fired a steady series of rounds into the chests of the three men in front of him, killing them instantly. There was only one way out and the two friends had no time for words. They put the pistols in their waistbands, picked up an AK-47 each and ran directly into the lobby, which is where all hell broke out.

Shots were fired from every direction. Tom, hit in the chest and his right shoulder, kept firing. Oleg was hit twice in his left leg and fell to the ground, but he also kept returning fire. With their AK's on full automatic, the two veteran agents emptied their rifles' magazines before going back to their pistols. They made it as far as the lobby's front desk and took refuge behind its flimsy structure that provided enough protection for them to take out more four more members of the squad that was sent to execute them. But there were just too many hostiles.

AK rounds shattered the desk with several rounds hitting the two friends. Oleg took shots in his chest and Tom to his torso. The shooting slowed and then all firing stopped. Tom reached out and put his hand on Oleg's shoulder. He smiled and said, "Thank you my old friend. I am sorry that I let this happen. I hoped you would not come, but I knew you would." Tom coughed several times, blood flowing from his mouth, looked at Oleg and with his last breath before he died he said, "The key is safe."

Oleg, coughing up blood himself, watched his friend die. His emotions ran from sorrow for Tom to the knowledge that his own life was about to end. He managed a painful laugh at Tom's final words, taking some comfort in the knowledge that his American friend safely secured the key. Oleg looked up to see a fully masked man approach with an AK-47 carefully aimed at him. The man calmly and coldly asked, "Where is the key?"

Oleg coughed up more blood, laughed again and told the assassin, "You will find it in hell." He managed enough strength to point the Grach at the man, who instinctively and unemotionally ended Oleg's life with one rifle shot to the head.

## Chapter 2

The ringing of his mobile phone shattered his REM sleep and he awoke immediately. He saw that his wife beside him had not budged. That was a good thing. He did not want to explain a call this early in the morning. "Hold" he said answering the phone as he got up from the bed in his expensive silk pajamas and walked into the large opulently appointed living room. He stood by the large window overlooking the streets of Ostozhenka, the neighborhood known as Moscow's Golden Mile. One of the most expensive neighborhoods in the world, Ostozhenka has it all; opera, museums, fine restaurants and high end fashion. It is all here in the center of Moscow and it is all within a short walk of his luxurious apartment. High above this special district and on the phone to an unlikely confederate was the sole owner and chief executive officer of Enerprov, Andrei Chekhov.

Enerprov is the largest privately held oil and natural gas producer in the Russian Federation. The company's net worth is in the billions of U.S. dollars and many analysts agree that its untapped energy reserves, once fully proven, will double or triple Enerprov's value. The company was founded in 1989, just before the Soviet Union completely collapsed in 1991, by Viktor Chekhov. Viktor was a questionable figure who emerged from the Soviet black market with the friendship of many high placed government officials in the new Russian Federation. Those well positioned relationships help Viktor take Enerprov on a meteoric rise, obtaining and developing some of the richest energy acreage in Russia.

Over the next twenty years, the company successfully expanded its reach into the North Sea and Asia. There was little opposition to the firm's growth, especially with the unprecedented access it was always able to secure to U.S. energy industry science and engineering. Easy access to advanced seismic mapping, horizontal drilling and other exploration and production technology came with the full support of the U.S. government. Access to this technology clearly helped the company win approval from the Russian Federation for private ownership of some of the richest undeveloped energy fields in Russia.

Viktor was healthy and active at seventy-two years of age when he died mysteriously three years ago. Many in the industry thought that the Russian Federation would step in and slowly take control of his company but Viktor's son, Andrei, took over the company and further accelerated its success. Andrei, forty-eight years of age, was certainly his father's son.

Andrei started working at his father's side directly upon graduation from The Moscow Institute for Physics and Technology with a degree in geology. He worked under Viktor's tutorage for the next twenty-three years, right up the minute his father died, without missing a single day. He also had not taken any significant time off for the past three years since Viktor's death. Viktor was extremely tough on Andrei, the oldest of his four children and his only son. There wasn't anything that Andrei accomplished, regardless of how successful, that his father would praise. Success was expected, nothing more and nothing less. Andrei's need for Viktor's approval resulted in Andrei being involved in all of Enerprov's more controversial business dealings, but even making those questionable deals produce significant results did not impress Viktor. Success was expected.

A bear of a man, Andrei cares more about the company than anything else in his life. He keeps his beautiful wife and three daughters sheltered from the business and he loves his family. However, he also does not hesitate to use them as decorations when it is necessary for appearances. Clearly Andrei's true love is Enerprov.

From the time Andrei joined the company, Viktor shared with his son a plan that he and an American partner first visualized in 1978. The plan changed over the years and had fully formed just prior to Viktor's death. That plan, Viktor's plan, is now a mission, and the mission is Andrei's responsibility. Andrei still seeks his father's approval; approval that will never be granted in this life. Andrei listened intently to what the caller had to say.

"They killed ten of my best men!" the caller exclaimed, sounding annoyed at what was supposed to be easier - not easy, but easier. "I could care less about that idiot in the suit, but if you need to count him, then eleven dead on our side," the voice said.

"Please, spare me. The key, did you get the key and are the subjects dead?" he asked the caller.

"No sir, we did not get the key. However, both Oleg and the American are dead."

"Half a job is not half success. It is ALL failure!" he shouted at the caller, then lowered his voice remembering his wife and daughters were asleep in their bedrooms across the apartment. "What happened?" he continued.

"They were older but still deadly. We had little time for conversation. I did not want to risk either of them escaping. I did what had to be done," the caller said.

"Fine, I am not happy. But I understand. Did you clean up the area?"

"Not enough time. It was a loud firefight and we heard the police sirens, so we quickly left the building. I did not want to leave our dead, but we had no choice. No one had any identification. It will take the authorities weeks or more to figure out who the men were. I will touch base with the local police officials after dawn and make sure they remember who fills those envelopes with cash and caution them to slow the investigation as much as possible. I will instruct them to report the deaths as criminal acts and nothing more."

"The Key? What is your next step about finding it?"

"I know that Oleg has a daughter. My source says she is also FSB, so I will need to be careful. I am also told that she has no clue. My source assures me that Oleg would not have been so careless as to involve his daughter. I think you should follow up with your American partner," the caller said.

"Yes, I think you are right and I will make that call. You make sure all is good with the police and focus on the larger mission. With the two agents dead, there is no one who could get in our way. Don't fail the larger mission. We will only have this one chance after all these years," he said and cut off the call before any response from the caller.

Andrei gazed again through the window at the streets of Ostozhenka and thought about the situation. Everything was coming together. He needed to make sure that there would be nothing that would tie his family, his American partner or his company to what was about to unfold. The only two men who could have made trouble are now dead, but the recent rumor that one of the murdered agents might have set aside some evidence was haunting him. Did they really have photographs, or notes, or other materials? Perhaps there was nothing at all? But there was the recent talk of a key, a key to a box, a box that contains something. What key? What Box? What something? He felt the anxiety over the possibility of some piece of definitive evidence that could topple all that his father planned and all that they built together. No, the mission will be successful. With the objectives achieved, any evidence will be destroyed or certainly ignored. Andrei was sure that once he succeeded, Viktor would finally be proud of him.

He looked at the time, 5:00 a.m. in Moscow. It would be 8:00 p.m. in Washington D.C. He entered the number. The phone on the other end rang three times and then a familiar voice answered, "Andrei? Is that you? A little early in Moscow, isn't it?"

"Yes, yes it is me and it is early. How are you?"

"I am fine, finishing up one of those horribly boring dinners. Still; had to go; duty calls as they say!

How are Nadya and the girls? You know those girls are as dear to me as my own grandchildren. Your father and I were that close."

"They are all fine and I too think of you as family. Thank you for that. I have some news. The two problems have been taken care of," Andrei said.

"Excellent. They were the only direct link to your late father and me. With them out of the way, the road is clear," the voice responded quietly, almost in a whisper.

"I do have a question. A few weeks ago I heard from people I know, people connected to my more secretive helpers, about a box. They said that this box could be a problem," Andrei explained, without being more specific while speaking on a mobile phone. "I was also told of a key, a key that opens this box. My people, who solved the problems tonight, found neither. I thought you should know aware of the rumor, but I think it is nothing that we need to be concerned about," he added.

There was a pause for what seemed to be hours, but it was only a few seconds. "Box? Key? No, don't worry about that. I am sure it is nothing. You handled what needed to be handled. Your father would be proud," the voice said and continued, "Forget the rumor. We only to execute as planned. Oh, I hear my wife. Sounds like I need to shake some hands. I must go. Take care Andrei," he said, and he ended the call.

Andrei wasn't sure what to think. He was concerned about the existence of evidence, of this box and key. Though he was confident that it would not matter once the mission succeeded, he still worried if both he and his American partner were right about ignoring the rumor. Are they overlooking what could be a serious problem? Andrei was troubled but decided that there is nothing to do now but make sure the mission is accomplished. He looked at the clock on the bookcase across from the window and saw the time. He decided to get another hour of sleep.

Back in D.C., his wife of thirty-five years was not calling, though she was in the next room. Denise is an elegant woman. Her family, like his, is extremely wealthy. She, unlike him, had a sense of things greater than herself. He wanted power and position. She knew about his ambitious character from the first day they were introduced, but she signed on for the long haul. She understood that power was his greatest love, but she chose to be by his side and that was that. But she was not calling him to shake any more hands this evening. She was not calling him at all. He was disturbed about what Andrei told him and wanted to end the call without saying anything further.

He was worried about the rumor of the key and box, but there was no turning back now. There was no point in telling Andrei that he was concerned to hear about possible evidence. There is little that could be done at this point, and he had no other information. His choice was to ignore it and go forward. He stopped thinking about the mission and everything connected to it when Denise entered the room. She told him that the car was ready to take them home from the White House, where they were guests for a state dinner.

"Are you and Mrs. Harris ready to leave Mr. Speaker?" the young secret service agent asked the Speaker of the House.

"Yes, let's go" he smiled. Then Speaker James Harris took Denise's hand and followed the agent to the waiting limousine.

Andrei tried to go back to sleep, but found it difficult and decided he would catch up on some reading before going to the office. He read for an hour then showered, dressed and left the apartment to meet his driver at the usual time in front of the building. The drive to Enerprov's headquarters took only a few minutes. As soon as Andrei arrived, he began a long day that did not conclude until late in the evening with a scheduled business dinner.

When his day was finally done, it was already past 10:00 p.m. in Moscow. Andrei, in the car and on his way home, thought about Enerprov's unexpected opportunity to purchase U.S. energy assets. The potential deal was introduced to him only one week ago and already news of the possible acquisition resulted in some negative political reaction, so it was time to call his friend Peter Jenkins and let him know that Enerprov needs Bricksen Grove. "It is 1:00 p.m. in New York and Peter is most likely still at some important lunch," Andrei thought to himself. "All of Peter's lunches are important. He does his best work in those settings," Andrei thought as he laughed a little. Andrei has witnessed Peter working a table of guests over lunch and respects Peter's strong people skills. He decided to wait and call Peter in a few hours.

Andrei was ready for bed when he called Peter and asked him to set Bricksen Grove in motion on the acquisition. The conversation about the deal did not have the normal rush of excitement for Andrei. He could not ignore the opportunity to acquire U.S. assets, but even that milestone will be nothing compared to the success that will be achieved with his father's old plan.

## Chapter 3

New York City's Manhattan Borough is never bothered by winter. Snow may fall for hours and mess up the commute, but in no time at all the snow is plowed off its midtown streets, loaded into trucks and, depending on which side of the city from which the snow was removed, dumped into either the Hudson or East River. Crowds of people quickly return to freshly cleared sidewalks and go about their morning routine. They proudly display logo imprinted paper cups of high-end coffee and walk purposely into majestic towers of commerce to start their day.

A seventy story rectangular skyscraper of smoked glass and steel, located on Park Avenue just blocks north of the historic Waldorf Astoria hotel, is home to the headquarters of Bricksen, Grove & Alexander. Bricksen Grove, as it is always referred to, is a leading global management consulting firm whose clients include many sovereign governments and most of the major corporations on the planet. Occupying the top twenty floors, Bricksen Grove's offices are filled with activity twenty-four hours a day, seven days a week. The firm's leadership was especially busy this morning.

All ten members of the Partnership Council were in the building before 8:00 a.m. and gathered in the firm's spacious and opulently appointed board room located on the building's seventieth floor. The view from the wall of floor-to-ceiling windows was breathtaking, but no one was enjoying it. The seven men and two women sitting around the large marble table in the center of room were all focused on the tenth member of the Council, and Bricksen Grove's chief executive officer, Peter Jenkins. Peter, a tall man of sixty-three years of age and a stereotypical executive presence, stood at the head of table pointing to information displayed on a large flat panel monitor that was lowered from an enclosure in the ceiling.

"Enerprov is ready to move. Andrei Chekhov called me yesterday afternoon and he wants our help and he needs us to act quickly," Peter explained.

Bricksen Grove was first engaged by Enerprov ten years ago to advise on the merger of a number of its production subsidiaries into a single unit. Peter Jenkins handled most of the work himself and developed a working relationship with both Viktor and Andrei. Since Viktor's death, Andrei relied on Peter, fifteen years older than Andrei, as more than just a business advisor. It was not unusual for Andrei to speak with Peter about family matters as well as business.

Yesterday's call was all business. Enerprov's opportunity to acquire oil and natural gas rich acreage in Texas and Louisiana was important. These would be the first domestic U.S. energy fields that the company would own and Andrei wanted Bricksen Grove to help navigate the political and regulatory waters. The deal came to Enerprov unsolicited and Andrei jumped at the chance to own U.S. based assets. A firestorm of political posturing immediately followed after news of the possible acquisition hit the media, and Andrei immediately knew he wanted the influence of Bricksen Grove on his side.

"This is going to be tricky," Peter said to the Council. "Enerprov has great lawyers here in the United States, but they are going to need our connections and knowledge of the State Department. Even with Enerprov's many friends in our government, Andrei knows this is going to be uphill all the way and combining our contacts will help lessen the slope," Peter explained.

Bricksen Grove often engaged in assignments where the greatest strength brought by the firm was its influence and ability to leverage its government connections for the benefit of its clients. The purchase of U.S. based energy assets by a privately owned foreign enterprise is a complex transaction involving a number of laws and regulations. The acquisition of energy fields in the United States by a company owned by a citizen of a former cold war adversary has additional political and public relation hurdles, all of which need careful handling. Accomplishing this will require more than only adhering to law. One wrong move and public reaction could delay the transaction for years or possibly stop it in its tracks. It is therefore good business to engage the advice of a respected firm like Bricksen Grove to help on a person-to-person basis.

"Senator Thomson from Texas has already said publically that he will do everything he can to stop the sale of these assets to Enerprov," Peter told his partners. "The Senator's brief remarks are only the opening volley. You can be sure future comments will be more inflammatory," he added.

Mary Thomas, a well-dressed and professionally mannered career woman of fifty who has been with Bricksen Grove since her graduation from Yale, spoke up immediately, "We will show how this acquisition will bring fresh capital into our country and how this transaction will strengthen the job picture for American workers." Mary rose through the ranks and became one of the firm's first female partners and then the first female member of the Partnership Council. Physically attractive and incredibly smart, she chose business over family. Married, divorced and no children, she manages Bricksen Grove's Government Relations practice. "Peter, my division will go to work immediately on the politics," she added.

"Thank you Mary," Peter responded and then spoke directly to the head of the firm's Energy Industry practice, Donald Spencer, "Spence, what do you think?"

Donald Spencer grew up in the oil business in Texas, starting as a rig hand working the summers of his college years at the University of Texas. He went on to build a thirty-year career in the oil business before joining Bricksen Grove five years ago to take over its Energy Industry practice. "Well," he started in his distinctive Southwestern accent, "We have to first find out who all here in the U.S. of A. will want to take a shot at playing white knight and step out in front of Enerprov. Such a player could offer more money, or value of some kind, to take the deal from Enerprov. Politics will play a role and Enerprov will be left empty handed. Once we determine who the likely bidders are, we can figure out the best way for our client to structure the transaction to shut down all potential competitive offers. I already have a few ideas on who might be probable competitors. My people will handle this."

"Good," Peter said. "Mary and Spence have this. I will interface directly with Andrei, so let's get to it." Peter concluded the meeting and the room started to empty. Peter, Mary and Spence stood together and spoke among themselves for a few minutes before leaving the board room.

Hours earlier, three time zones and 3,500 miles across the Atlantic Ocean, Michael Clark was pacing slowly along the approach roadway and out of sight of the entrance to the British Airways terminal at London's Heathrow International Airport. It was late in the evening in London and Michael had already checked his bag with the lone attendant on duty at the far end of the terminal. His flight to New York was on time to depart in an hour, but he had another appointment first.

At five feet, ten inches tall and all of 160 pounds, Michael was a figure of fitness. His thin facial features and muscular stature hide the fact that this handsome man is fifty-six years of age, but his full head of graying hair and lines in his face do show the reality of time. He was wearing a neat blue business suit, no tie, and an opened black dress coat.

It is never easy for Michael to be in or around a major airport. Before long, he always starts to think about his beautiful wife, Sharon, and his eight year old angelic little daughter, Cindy. He thinks about how their innocent lives were mercilessly taken by terrorists who attacked Rome's Fiumicino-Leonardo da Vinci International Airport twenty-two years ago. Michael tried to fight the memory by checking the time on his wristwatch and looking at the terminal's outside facade but his thoughts returned to his family. He had just completed a mission in command of a unit in the 5th Special Forces Group of the United States Army during the Desert Storm operation of the Gulf War in 1991, and he was on leave. He arranged to meet his wife and daughter for a week in Rome. Their plane landed several hours before Michael's plane was scheduled to arrive, and the plan was for Sharon and Cindy to check into the hotel, relax and wait for Michael. They never made it.

Six Middle Eastern Islamic terrorists armed with automatic weapons, shot their way into the airport's main arrival terminal with the intent of hurting as many innocent people as they could. Italian security teams, stationed at the airport and on alert during the Gulf War, eventually killed all the terrorists. In only a few horrifying minutes, ten civilians and three security officers were murdered with many other innocents and security personnel wounded. Michael's wife and daughter were unfortunately among the dead.

For a man as disciplined, as tough and as combat hardened as he, Michael cannot control his thoughts about his lost family. He starred at the terminal and fought back his overwhelming emotions. His heart will never heal from the lost promise of what could have been for Cindy, and his love for Sharon is as strong today as it was on their wedding day. He never remarried and always wears his wedding ring on a chain around his neck, keeping it close to his heart.

Thankfully, the sound of a car's engine interrupted Michael's thoughts. He watched as a black cab pulled close to the terminal and stopped. The cab immediately drove off after a man, dressed in business attire, exited. This was the man for whom Michael was waiting. The outside of the terminal was quiet after the cab left and only thirty feet separated the two men when suddenly the high pitched whine of motor bike engines broke the silence. One bike quickly appeared from around the bend leading to the terminal and was shortly joined by a second bike. The man who exited the cab ran up to Michael, handed him a flash drive and kept running away from the terminal.

Both riders aimed their bikes for Michael and accelerated toward him. Michael braced himself as he slowly reached for the collapsible metal baton strapped above his right ankle. Just as the first bike reached him, Michael snapped open the baton and smashed it through the face guard of the rider's helmet. The man hit the ground hard with his bike spinning away. The rider on the second bike had to quickly slow and turn out of the way of the fallen bike, which gave Michael enough time to retrieve the baton from the unconscious rider's bloody face guard.

As the second bike turned and charged, Michael timed a fall to the ground and jammed the baton into the bike's chain drive. The bike bucked uncontrollably, throwing its rider ten feet forward and down, hard, onto the pavement. Michael stood up, saw the second unconscious rider on the ground, brushed off his coat and walked slowly to the terminal's entrance, tossing the baton into a trash bin. He proceeded to his gate and calmly walked through security in time to join the other travelers boarding the late flight to New York.

Several floors below the seventieth floor board room, on a more modestly furnished floor; the Corporate Security practice of Bricksen Grove is housed. The lights in Michael's small office were still turned off, as Michael walked from the elevator at 9:00 a.m. He was sipping an everyman's coffee that he purchased from a nearby take-out restaurant, which does a brisk breakfast business selling bagels and fresh brewed plain and simple coffee. Michael's flight from London experienced some delays and arrived at John F. Kennedy International Airport in New York hours later than scheduled. As a result, Michael did not get to his Manhattan apartment until midnight. He caught a few hours of sleep, awoke early and wrestled with taking Friday off, but decided to come to the office and catch up on some overdue paperwork.

Michael's engagement in London was for a major financial firm, a long time Bricksen Grove client that was concerned about protecting their executives while they attended business meetings in certain countries. It was a routine engagement. Michael met with the client's security executives and recommended procedures and resources to be employed to keep their people safe while in troubled countries. A routine engagement for Michael, one of Bricksen Grove's most requested security consultants. Intercepting the flash drive was Michael's extra-curricular activity, one that he performed as an independent contractor for the CIA. His global travel for Bricksen Grove was the perfect cover for his secret life.

"Good Morning Mike," called Peter Jenkins as he walked to Michael's office. "I was told you would be back this morning and wanted to come down and say thank you for another job well done," Peter added. Peter really liked Michael. The fact that they were close in age was a helpful reminder that the firm does have some mature staff among its legions of thirty-year olds who, though they may be the smartest of their generation, were largely a highly combustible mix of hormones and ambition. There was also something about Michael's demeanor and overall presence that Peter enjoyed being near. Peter had no idea about Michael's work for the CIA.

"How was London?" he asked.

"Wet!" Michael answered. "The client was great and I did enjoy the week, all kidding aside about the lousy weather," he added.

"Well, it is good to have you back in New York. You should have taken the day off," Peter said. This comment made Michael smile since earlier he was thinking the same thing. "It is Friday, so go home early tonight and do something fun this weekend," Peter said, shaking Michael's hand. He then walked away.

Suddenly, Michael's mobile phone rang. "Michael Clark," he said.

"It's Dave, Mike. We have a serious problem. The Agency needs your help. Are you up for another assignment so soon?" The voice on the other end of the call was that of David Capella, Michaels' handler at the CIA. Michael started free-lancing for the CIA since leaving the Army twenty years ago. Was this a secret life? Maybe it was? Why? He needed to keep active and he needed to put himself between his country and its enemies. Compensating for not being in the airport terminal when his family was murdered? Yes. Was there any way that he could have been at the airport with his family? No. Does that really matter? No. This is his life now and he intends to stay active as long as he can help stop more death, destruction and anyone who threatens the innocent.

"I am," Michael replied.

"Thank you Mike, I am in New York today. Please meet me for coffee at the Waldorf in fifteen minutes," David said. The phone call ended.

## Chapter 4

David Capella is a tall man of average build. The wrinkles in his face and his receding hair line showed his age, but also gave him a look of gravitas. Gravitas his decades of experience had earned. He recently turned sixty and has enough years of service to retire comfortably. Retirement is analogous to suicide for David, so he never gives it any serious consideration. This morning his eyes, partially shielded by his wire framed glasses, are unusually bloodshot. Sleep is also something foreign to David, but the past thirty-six hours were unusually troubling. Fortunately the rich aroma of his coffee followed by its deep rich taste and its plentiful caffeine provided him with a strong enough second wind to be alert for his meeting with Michael. He sipped his coffee slowly as he observed the people in both the restaurant and in the Waldorf's main lobby. The open format restaurant, with no walls, is in the center of lobby.

He watched the young waitress who would smile affectionately every time she approached a customer. He listened to the exaggerated French accent of the hostess who, though probably from France, has most likely been in New York since she was a young child. Still, the accent impressed the many international customers served by the restaurant. David is the farthest from being a bigoted man of any kind, but his years of investigative instinct forced him to wonder if many of the bus boys were in the country legally or not. Then there are all the customers, the hotel guests checking in and checking out and all the others passing through or meeting contacts. The setting is a perfect petri dish of the human fabric; a wonderful laboratory for a CIA professional.

Michael walked into the hotel using the revolving door from Park Avenue, up the marble staircase and through the front seating lounge into the main lobby. He immediately saw David over the barrier of low profile plant stands that provide a fortress line to delineate the restaurant's boundaries from the lobby. Michael approached the hostess and whispered that he is here to meet David, pointing to him. She was happy to accompany Michael to the table. "Thank you," Michael said. She smiled, turned and walked back to her post at the entrance to the restaurant area.

"Hey Dave" Michael said extending his hand.

"Morning, Mike," David responded, as he stood up and shook Michael's hand. "Sorry about the trouble at Heathrow. We cleaned it up. Both survived. Thank you for handling it."

"All in a day's work," Michael said, as he handed the flash drive to David who put it in his pocket.

The CIA piggybacks Michael's assignments on to his international consulting engagements. Typically they have him intercept a flash drive, disk or other media, usually loaded with sensitive data of some kind. Being an independent contractor, it is easy for him to serve as a drop for agents moving information. The agent, usually being followed, would pass the media to Michael and then continue to lead his followers on a fool's chase. Other times, Michael would engage a target driven to him by career agents and then extract the information being carried by the target. Those assignments were more physical and necessary depending on the circumstances. Sometimes those following the agent would see the exchange and pursue Michael, as was the case in London.

The use of an intercept provides the CIA with a great deal of flexibility. Michael's background, skill and international engagements make him a perfect nondescript player. He appears suddenly; either receives the media or takes it; then disappears.

"You look like you haven't had much sleep lately. What's up?" Michael asked David.

"Coffee, sir?" the young waitress asked with a warm smile as Michael sat down.

"Yes, please," Michael answered. She lifted the cup from the table, poured the fresh coffee and walked away.

"We have a major problem in a Moscow suburb, Mike. A city, a few miles east, called Reutov. This past Wednesday night our time, early Thursday morning Moscow time, a veteran agent of ours, Tom Moore, and his old friend Oleg Petrov were killed. Tom just retired and went to Moscow to celebrate with Oleg. Oleg was also a veteran agent, for them not us. He came up through the KGB and following the collapse of the Soviet Union and ultimately the KGB, he continued with the successor organization. That organization, as you know, is the Russian Federation's Federal Security Service or FSB. Even at his age, sixty-three, Tom was a threat. He was a hardened and capable agent. Oleg, a year older than Tom, was also tough as nails. Separately, neither man would be an easy target. Together, they would be a two man army. They had to have been attacked by an over-whelming force. Their bodies were riddled with 7.62 mm rounds," David paused, sipped some coffee and continued.

"The local police tell us that this appears to be a case of mistaken identity by a criminal mob. They said they will pursue the case, but could not guarantee an arrest."

Mike drank some coffee and said to David, "My guess is you don't trust the local police?"

"Hell No! Their investigation is pure bullshit. The say they found only Tom and Oleg, but my guess is that there were a pile of hostile bodies that were removed. Those bodies will show up in some morgue, or in several morgues, soon enough. Tom and Oleg were not easy marks and even though I am sure that they were attacked by a trained execution squad, they would have taken a number of their attackers with them. We are sure they were targeted, but we have no idea why."

"How do you see me helping?" Michael asked.

"Until we know whether or not it's open season on our agents, we need an independent to do some ground work in country. I know this is not a normal intercept assignment, but this is not a normal situation," David confessed to Michael.

"I hear that Bricksen Grove might be starting another engagement for Enerprov. I will see if I can get a brief engagement that would require me to be in Moscow. There is always a reason to review security and that review is always best started, if not completely satisfied, at a client's headquarters," Michael said. He added, "I am happy to help, Dave."

"Your usual rate will be paid to the usual account."

"I appreciate that, but this one is on me. I didn't know Tom Moore, but when a teammate is down, I can't profit from his death. I'm paid enough from Bricksen

Grove and I make great money from you guys on the intercepts."

You're a good man Mike. Call me as soon as you have the engagement and I will see if the Agency has any more information that will be useful to you."

Michael and David finished their coffee, traded a few more thoughts and after David paid the check, both men left the restaurant and the Waldorf.

Michael went back to his office and thought about how he would inject himself into the Enerprov transaction. He reviewed the public files to which he had access on the firm's client database. He found that the review of Enerprov security protocols had not been updated in years. This could be his opening. He called Peter's assistant and asked for a few minutes of Peter's time.

Marjorie Storm, Peter's assistant, has a heavy crush for Michael. She is a forty-six year old, tall athletic blond. Her brilliant blue eyes are hypnotic. In college, she was the homecoming queen and her ex-husband was the starting quarterback on the football team. They were a real life "Ken and Barbie" but then Ken turned out to be a real jerk and cheated on her. She divorced him and is happy being a single mom to her teenage daughter. Marjorie is organized, sharp and fiercely protective of her boss' time. All that said; Michael could come by whenever he wants. Since Peter also enjoys speaking with Michael, making some time on Peter's schedule for Michael is never a problem.

Michael walked into the executive area, and immediately made eye contact with Marjorie. Her smile and penetrating stare would melt a normal man, but Michael was a real challenge. "Hey Mike," she said, deepening her stare, "Welcome back from London. Do you have anything planned for the weekend?"

"Thank you Marj, no plans yet."

"My daughter has a sleepover with friends and I was going to try a new salmon recipe. I have enough for two?" she said. Marjorie knew what the answer was going to be, but she thought she would try. She's bound to get a yes to one of her constant invitations.

"Marj I would really like to accept, but I got back late from London. I would probably fall asleep, face first into the salmon. Perhaps some other time?" he said.

"Promise?"

"Yes, I promise," he said. She knew he would not keep the promise. The word around the office was that Michael was so much in love with the wife he lost, that even after all this time he still cannot have a committed affair with another woman. Everyone was sure that he has physical relations with women, but not anything that would be considered a serious relationship. Naturally that just made him more desirable and

Marjorie feels like a school girl whenever he is within twenty feet.

"Michael," Peter walked out, just in time to pull Michael out of Marjorie's presence and save her from fainting. Well, maybe.

The two men went into Peter's office and discussed the Enerprov account. Michael is not a partner but he is a senior consultant. He is also Peter's friend and can freely discuss any business engagement. He said to Peter that he heard about the possibility of another engagement with Enerprov and he did some homework, discovering that their security review was dated. Peter, knowing that he could trust Michael's discretion, shared with him that Enerprov was contemplating a U.S. acquisition. Michael suggested that understanding the clients' current security procedures and resources would be useful, as well as a necessary part of a due diligence disclosure to the seller. He said he would only need a few days in Moscow and had the entire coming week free. Peter agreed and said he would clear the trip with the client and that Michael should call the logistics group and set up the necessary clearance to go to Moscow as soon as next Tuesday for a three to four day engagement.

Marjorie watched Michael leave the area and get back on the elevator. She felt her heart rate increase and knew that tonight it will be difficult for her to sleep.

By the end of the day, everything was arranged with Enerprov and all the necessary travel permissions were secured for a brief visit to Moscow. Michael called David and told him everything was set and that he would plan on remaining in Moscow through the weekend, giving him up to six days to see what he could find out about what happened to Tom and Oleg.

David told Michael that once in Moscow he will be approached by an FSB agent who volunteered to help. He told him that the agent is Anya Petrova, Oleg's daughter. Michael asked David if that was a good idea. First, she was FSB. Second, the emotional attachment could be a problem.

David assured him that contacts high up in the FSB told him that the Service wanted to know what happened to Oleg as much as the CIA wanted to know what happened to Tom; especially since Oleg was still an active agent. David believed the sincerity of his sources. Anya, in the Service for the past three years, is an analyst and her expertise may prove useful. Also, she speaks perfect English versus the occasional Russian phrase that Michael is capable of muttering. They agreed that she would be helpful and then Michael asked the question, "How old is Anya?"

David hesitated and quietly said, "Twenty-five," as he braced for Michael's reaction.

"Are you out of your mind? She is a child! I have a few days in country to find out what the hell happened and you want me to baby sit? You're nuts!"

"Are you done?" David asked.

"No, yes, I don't know. This is crazy. She is young and she is the daughter of one of the murdered agents. Are you really sure about this Dave?"

"I am Mike. The FSB sees her as one of their rising stars. She is mature, capable and incredibly disciplined. She will be an asset."

"Okay," Michael said, taking a long breath before continuing, "I will keep an open mind and work with her. Do you have any solid intelligence that could serve as a starting point?" he asked.

David told Michael that Tom and Oleg met for the first time, in 1978 in Moscow. Oleg was assigned to protect a Soviet citizen, some important figure who was going to meet an American. The American, also some important person, had Tom assigned to accompany him.

Why did they meet? No records could be found. The only reason why the meeting was known was because there are a few retired agents who worked with

Tom and remembered Tom telling them how he met Oleg. Also, in the late 1970's there were many such meetings between citizens from both sides. It was all part of an effort to get to understand the other side. No records of these meetings were kept. They were not supposed to have taken place and were largely the work of internal KGB, at the time, and CIA brain trusts. The idea was similar to a game of 'chicken,' see if either side would provide something useful to the other. On occasion these meetings would produce some basis for a cooperative follow up, but those were a rare bi-product and usually by accident.

The meeting took place in a pub just one street away from the Lubyanka Station of the Moscow Metro. Oleg and Tom were together for hours at one table, while the citizens they were charged with protecting met across the pub at another table. Tom was fluent in Russian and Oleg fluent in English so they began a conversation of their own, trading languages, and by the end of the evening they developed a friendship.

Their friendship grew over the years. In 1983, while both were in Berlin. Tom and Oleg ran into each other in a bar on the West side of the Wall. Oleg was on personal business and Tom on assignment. After some drinks and conversation, Oleg said he was going to meet the woman who would become his wife and left the bar. Tom noticed that Oleg had forgotten a coin they were using to flip for drinks and Tom thought he would return it to Oleg.

He went outside to find four Afghan thugs holding long knives, surrounding Oleg. They were calling him an occupier and murderer of the Afghan people. Oleg had never been part of the Soviet War in Afghanistan, but he was Soviet and these assassins were in West Berlin to find Soviets soldiers on leave, or other Soviets, and murder them. Going into East Berlin would be too dangerous, so they would lay in wait for the occasional Soviet to enter the West for better quality drink and food.

Tom quickly saw the trouble and as soon as one of the attackers made a move, Tom grabbed him from behind. Within seconds, Tom and Oleg were standing over four dead would-be assassins and thirsty for more drinks. They decided to drink elsewhere.

It was only five years after that that Oleg and Tom celebrated Anya's birth.

The only other information that David had for Michael was an address, "Struska Street 16-25." The address is close to Lubyanka Station. The information was written on a piece of paper found in Tom's hotel room in Moscow, which the CIA was able to get to after the murders and before anyone else had access to Tom's room.

Michael had the date and place of a secret meeting that took place thirty-six years ago. He also had an address near the site of that meeting. This wasn't much, but it is a start. Working with the young daughter of one of the victims is going to add another layer of complexity and considering that there may be a concerted effort underway to execute both CIA and FSB agents, what can possibly make this assignment more difficult?

# Chapter 5

The city of Grozny, the capital of the Chechen Republic, is truly a phoenix. Almost completely destroyed during the First and Second Chechen Wars, the city's reconstruction has been epic. Modern architecture is rampant and Grozny is highlighted by many new, tall office and residential towers creating a breathtaking skyline. Businesses were reestablished and mass transportation rebuilt. The scars of the bitter conflict with Russia are less visible now on the steel and stone, but still noticeable when looking into the eyes of the Chechen people. The distrust of Russia, though widespread, it is not spoken about as much as in the recent past. A strong separatist movement lives on in this new city, as does a less political but just as strong under-world of organized crime. There is a fine line between the true Chechen patriot and the profiteering Chechen criminal. Viktor Chekhov was skilled at navigating this narrow line, a line that Andrei Chekhov has been struggling to manage on his own for the past three years.

The distance that separates Grozny from Moscow is eleven hundred miles but it might as well be eleven thousand miles as far as Andrei is concerned. Unlike his father, Andrei dislikes setting foot in the city, even though Enerprov has a trading and marketing operation that employs over three hundred Chechen citizens in Grozny. Viktor established the office shortly

41

after the Second Chechen War to assist in the recovery of the city. The business is real, but it could have easily been set up any place in the world. The operation in Grozny is Enerprov's way of extending some Russian outreach to the Chechen people. It also serves as a useful conduit to pay for those special services that that could only be provided by certain skilled workers, skilled workers like Rushad Umarov. Enerprov employs Rushad as a courier, but Andrei uses him for special assignments.

Rushad led the operation that murdered Tom and Oleg in Reutov and it was Rushad who shot Oleg at point blank range. It was all part of his current special assignment for Andrei. Rushad is a sinister man. He stands about six foot tall, is athletically built and a veteran of both Chechen Wars. At forty-eight he is an extremely bitter man filled with nothing but hate and rage. He hates the Russian Federation government completely, and he cares little for the average Russian citizen.

Rushad, despite his constant rationalization that all his misdoings are for Allah or at least in the name of Allah, uses his Muslim faith as a shill for his revenge. If he were truly a good Muslim and held real faith to Islam, then Rushad would have some remnant of a soul. But he has none. His wife and two young children were killed in bombing raids during the First Chechen War. His parents, his younger sister and her three children all died in bombing raids during the Second Chechen War. He cannot be reasoned with and will not listen to the fact that it was war; that Russian military were killed as well; and that innocent Russian civilians were bombed to death by terrorist actions during both of those wars. There is no reasoning with Rushad. The Russians killed his family and that is his only reality. The City of Grozny is being rebuilt with real substance beneath its shiny new exterior, but Rushad remains empty. He is a man with a core of hate who lacks respect for human life.

Rushad's current special assignment started over one year ago and is the implementation of Viktor's plan, now Andrei's mission. For Andrei, the reason for the mission is the achievement of power. This matters little to Rushad. For him, the mission will allow him to extract revenge on Russia. Andrei selected him for the mission because he knew that Rushad would do anything and everything necessary for success. He understands that all Rushad wants is revenge and his lust for that revenge will carry the mission to success, resulting in enormous power for Andrei.

Rushad accepts that he is being used by Andrei and that Andrei represents so much that he hates. No matter, a small price to pay for his revenge. He knows what is expected and, together with his cousin Halil Zakayev, followed Andrei's orders and organized the entire mission over the past year. Rushad and Halil firmly believe that this operation will be a statement to the Russian Federation and to the world, that the Chechen people do not forget and demand justice. The Chechen people want more control of their own lives and they desire to make Islam dominant in their government. This mission will accomplish it all. If Andrei profits from it, so be it. He is paying for the operation. The line between patriot and criminal was never so thin.

Halil was educated as an aeronautical engineer with a specialty in mechanical engineering. He is employed by Enerprov for his skill set in mechanical engineering. But his true genius is his ability to take any technical design, aeronautical or mechanical, and modify that design to perform differently than its original intent. He has used this ability to adapt American oil production technology to Enerprov's specific requirements. Halil is pleased to use these same talents to serve the Chechen cause. Rushad, on the other hand, is completely consumed by hate and is focused purely on revenge.

The mission's objective is to eliminate targets in two cities five thousand miles apart. To accomplish this objective, all of Halil's engineering training and talents were necessary. He secured three standard Russian ZALA 421-12 surveillance drones, with Andrei's financial support and Enerprov's military connections. With a wing span of two meters and a total weight of approximately four kilograms, these unmanned aerial vehicles could carry an additional kilogram of payload and remain fast and agile enough to be difficult to detect. Powered by an electric motor and an integral battery pack, launch preparation requires less than three minutes.

Halil's design changes to these drones were elegant. He modified these normally non-lethal machines to hold a small laser guided missile that is no larger than the surveillance cameras the drones were originally designed to carry. Each missile has enough power to deliver a small explosive that when placed within one foot of its target, will be enough to kill three men. Each drone will be flown from a distance of about ten miles from the target area, taking it about thirty minutes to reach its destination and acquire its target. Painting the target area with a laser Halil fitted into its nose cone, the drone will be directed to dive toward the target. The missile will be fired as the dive starts. The deadly device will accelerate many times the decent speed of the drone, following the laser line to the target.

The combination of surprise from the speed of the missile and its accurate placement will more than make up for the small explosive payload. Each target will be eliminated.

The targets will be hit simultaneously, but a world apart. One target is in Moscow and the other two in Washington, D.C. To help ensure that the drones are not detected until it is too late to protect against them, a diversion is planned. The diversion is a little more conventional. A sleeper cell, in place near each city, trained to help with the drones will also assemble a small bomb to be detonated in a busy commuting area. The explosions will be minor but loud. The noise will create panic and each explosion will also release lethal gas from an attached canister to extend the death toll and extend the fear.

Even with the gas, the death toll will be minimal. However, the panic will be high and difficult to control quickly. Since the placement of these bombs will be within a mile of the main targets, response will momentarily draw attention from the target areas. At that moment, the drones will have already started their decent.

The mission is ready to be executed one week from Monday. One bomb, one drone, one missile for Moscow, while the second set, including a second missile equipped drone, for Washington D.C. The Moscow event will take placc at 6:30 p.m. local time.

Simultaneously the second event will occur at 9:30 a.m. on the same day in Washington, D.C. Each drone will be launched precisely thirty minutes prior to the detonation of the bombs, allowing the drones to be positioned to attack at exactly the beginning of the chaos resulting from the bombs.

Rushad will set up in Reutov. Halil will set up in Landover, Maryland, eight miles north of D.C. The sleeper cells have been in place for years and in recent months have been receiving all the materials and equipment necessary. The cell members, remaining apart from each other, followed directions embedded in various websites on the Internet, taking turns to assemble the drones, missiles and bombs. It will all be ready. Rushad and Halil plan to arrive at their respective posts a few days prior to the attacks. The plan is in motion and the mission will succeed.

Sunday evening in his apartment in Ostozhenka, Andrei was thinking about his father. He walked to the small framed Picasso print on the wall, beside the dark cherry desk in his study. The frame was hinged to the wall and Andrei opened it like a door. Behind the print was a wall safe. He entered the digital code and opened the safe door. He reached into the safe and removed an old leather bound notebook and then sat down behind the desk and turned the pages of the notebook to an entry made in November of 1978. His father's hand writing was neat and the entry's message was crystal clear. Andrei read the Russian language notes and smiled. How could his father and James Harris have planned all this thirty-six years ago? How could they have been so dedicated to the plan and so disciplined, that they shaped their entire lives to make sure the plan would have an opportunity to succeed? Regardless how, they did. With Viktor gone, it was now up to Andrei to carry out his father's dream; his father's grand plan.

## Chapter 6

Moscow has a number of airports, but most of the traffic is handled by its three major airports located in a ring around the center of the city. These airports, Demodedovo, Sheremetyevo and Vnukovo have been modernized and all three are busy. Sheremetyevo, the hub of the Russian international airline Aeroflot, handled over 26 million passengers and 230,000 airline movements in 2012. It was made famous, or infamous, when U.S. National Security Agency independent contractor Edward Snowden arrived there in the summer of 2013. Sheremetyevo is a busy modern airport with enough intrigue for anyone.

Michael traveled through Sheremetyevo many times, but this time he was the guest of Enerprov. A waiting chauffeured ZIL limousine and complementary booking in one of the thirty-one luxurious suites of the small but elegant Kebur Palace Hotel in Moscow's Ostozhenka district, certainly was indicative of his host's flair for the opulent. The kind smile of the driver, holding a sign with Michael's last name neatly printed on it, made so much of a welcoming impression that Michael almost didn't think about his wife and daughter as he exited the airport - almost.

The comfortable limousine, with plenty of vodka, still couldn't make the horrible Moscow traffic any easier. This grand city is not designed for modern vehicle traffic. The Metro system is the best way to travel from Sheremetyevo Airport to any city location, but not when you are the guest of Enerprov. Michael was completely relaxed in the rear seat of the ZIL and actually enjoyed the stop and go drive. It was Tuesday evening in Moscow and he was looking forward to a restful night before he tackles his business engagement for Bricksen Grove and then his work for the CIA.

A bellman approached the limousine after it pulled to a stop in front of the Kebur Palace Hotel. He took Michael's bag from the trunk, the lid to which had been remotely opened by the driver. The driver quickly raced around the car to open Michael's door. Michael, business suit and no tie, thought about how easily he could get used to this treatment.

As he walked into the hotel's small but richly appointed lobby, its warmth was immediately inviting and a pleasant contrast to the massive cathedral style lobbies of the major hotels. Michael stopped at the front desk where he was greeted by an incredibly beautiful young woman who spoke perfect English. She asked for Michael's passport while smiling with her deep blue eyes, as much as with her model-like lips. "Could heaven be any more inviting?" Michael thought to himself.

"I see you will be with us for six nights, Mr. Clark? We do hope you enjoy your stay. All expenses you incur in our hotel: your room, meals and any services or purchases, are the complements of Enerprov. You are in room 316. Please call the front desk if you need anything and enjoy your time with us and in Moscow, Mr. Clark," she said in a voice so soft and inviting that Michael stood motionlessly for a few seconds and allowed her words to gently pass through his brain.

"Thank you, my Russian is not very good but I believe the name on your badge would be "Irina" in English? So thank you Irina," Michael responded.

"Why, that is correct, Mr. Clark," she answered with another soul piercing look from those endless pools of blue that she was using for eyes. "Gosh, she is beautiful," Michael thought, as he smiled shyly and followed the bellman to the elevator.

A short walk from the elevator, after arriving at the third floor, the bellmen opened the door to Room 316. The suite's spacious and beautiful interior made an immediate positive impression. Michael could not help but feel comfortable. The kind driver, the limousine, the helpful bellman, the drop dead gorgeous woman at the front desk and this elegant room combined to provide Michael with a warm Moscow welcome?

He saw a silver tray with a silver bucket of ice holding a bottle of champagne, French of course, on the table behind a small upholstered loveseat. He picked up the tent card, opening it to reveal a note printed in English, "I am looking forward to meeting you at our offices tomorrow, Mr. Clark. Your suggestion to perform a security review on the front-end of this transaction was pure brilliance. Not only will it save us time, but it will also show all concerned that Enerprov is the right partner for any American business. Enjoy the champagne. We expect to see you at 9:00 a.m. tomorrow, Andrei Chekhov" the note read.

Michael smiled, opened the chilled champagne and filled one of the two tall crystal flutes that were next to the bucket on the tray. He had enough time to take a long sip before his mobile phone buzzed the arrival of a text message that read, "Meet me in the lobby. I am wearing a red dress, Anya"

"Okay, Dave provided my number to her and now it is time to go to work and baby sit," Michael thought to himself, still not sure that having this young woman work with him was a good idea. He swallowed the remaining champagne in the flute and left his room for the elevator.

Michael stepped from the elevator into the lobby and he looked around for a young woman wearing a red dress. He wasn't sure what to expect and certainly not prepared for who walked toward him. She was petite and shapely with lush shoulder length black hair. Her brown eyes were captivating and revealed an innocent soul. This young woman was not just beautiful on the outside, but possessive of a presence that could only be described as holy. How could she possibly be with the FSB, even as an analyst?

"Mr. Clark?" she asked.

"I am Michael Clark" he answered.

"I am Anya. I have reservations for dinner a short walk from here. It is a quiet place with good food. We can talk there without raising any questions. Yes, questions. I am dressed in this short cocktail dress so that Enerprov's surveillance person will think that you arranged for me to meet you. You know, a service provided by the hotel and paid for by yourself, nice and discrete," she said in solid English encrusted in a heavy Russian accent.

"Okay," Michael said and then thought about how stupid he sounded. What the hell? This young woman is stunning but her age is less than the difference in their ages. He felt like a fool on so many levels but swallowed his pride and helped her with her coat. He accepted her arm and walked with her through the hotel entrance.

As they strolled the few minutes to the restaurant, Anya pointed out some of the district's sites. Her conversation was pleasant and interesting, though he felt that she was observing his reactions as much as she was informing him about the city. She did make obvious gestures in a manner expected by the man Enerprov sent to follow Michael.

They reached a small restaurant that was filled with a mix of Moscow's business and societal elite. The crowd was predominantly Russian but from the scattering of other languages being spoken, the international flare of this part of the city was obvious. Michael and Anya would blend in well. She picked a perfect place for them to get acquainted and share information.

An attractive mature woman with an aura of success greeted them inside the entrance and showed them to their table. The woman spoke in Russian and asked some questions to which Anya responded in a pleasant and friendly tone. Michael understood some of the conversation and recognized it as polite small talk. He did hear his name mentioned and at that point the woman turned to him and in English said, "Welcome to Moscow. I do hope that you will enjoy your dinner in my little restaurant as well as your entire stay in our city. Let me take your coats."

Michael helped Anya with her coat, removed his and handed both coats to the woman. She, in turn, handed them to a pretty young woman who took the coats to the check room. Michael thanked the owner and told her he was looking forward to both dinner and his time in Moscow. She asked him if this was his first visit and he was proud to say he had been to Moscow before, but he told her that this was his first time to this elegant part of the city. The woman explained that when she first opened the restaurant, the Ostozhenka district was less than what it is today and how she was fortunate to be part of the neighborhood's growth. She smiled, offered to help with anything they needed, wished them a good dinner and walked back to greet other arriving guests.

"It is not unusual to see women owners of her age in Moscow," Anya said to Michael. "My father taught me that Russian women, who had to play a larger role in society because of all the men who died in World War II, raised their daughters to be the strongest and most aggressive women in the world today. The owner of this restaurant is an example of those daughters. She is of that strong generation. I believe that is your generation, if I may say? She is quite impressive. I want to be like her." Anya added.

The waiter came by and asked if they would like a drink. Anya ordered a glass of chardonnay and Michael joined her. Anya translated the menu for Michael and when the waiter returned with their wine, she helped him order. The waiter thanked them and said he would be back with their first course. Anya and Michael made a toast to a new friendship and sipped some wine and then Anya really surprised him.

"Alright, Mr. Clark, what is her name?" She asked.

"Whose name?" he answered.

"The woman you love. I may be young, but I learned enough about older men to know how they look at young women who take their arms and flirt with them. You are not showing any interest. In fact, you look uncomfortable. I think I am quite beautiful this evening, so it is obviously not me," she laughed a little and continued, "So my analysis is that you are a man in love."

"Well Anya, you are right on all your points. I will begin by saying that I agree with you in that you are extremely beautiful and yes, I am a little uncomfortable. I was blessed with a wonderful daughter who would be thirty years old now, only five years older than I was told is my "hired date" for tonight." He paused as his "hired date" comment made them both smile. "I also had a great wife. We were deeply in love and I love her even more today. Tragically, both my wife and my daughter were killed twenty-two years ago," he said.

"I am sorry," Anya said as her demeanor changed to a more serious tone. "I had no idea. The profile on you that I was provided by the Service did not mention anything about the loss of your family. I can see the love you still have for your wife and I see the pride in your eyes when you speak of your daughter. I know that my father was proud of me and that knowledge is comforting to me as I think of him. As for the love you have for your wife that still burns in your heart, I can only pray that someday a man will love me as much," she added, as she reached out and touched Michael's hand.

"Anya, I am sure that the lucky man who wins your heart will be worthy. You impress me as a woman who would accept no less."

"Thank you for that," Anya replied.

The ice was broken and they continued to learn more about each other, as any two new friends would, while they enjoyed the fine cuisine of the restaurant. Enerprov's man, who followed them into the restaurant and went directly into the bar to maintain his surveillance, began to lose interest in the boring couple he was assigned to observe.

When coffee arrived, Michael turned the conversation to business and asked Anya, "Tell me about your father's relationship with Tom Moore."

She told him about the long friendship and how the two rival agents were as close as brothers. Anya said that each man would lay down his life for the other. She met Tom Moore when she was only seven years old. She always called him 'Uncle' and she loved him as one would love an uncle. She told Michael that investigators in the FSB examined the bodies and noticed marks on Tom's wrists. The Service was sure that he had been restrained. Their theory is that Oleg was lured into a trap to help his friend, his brother. She said that Oleg was former KGB and even though he had not had a field assignment in the past year, he had to know that he was headed into a trap. Still, he went. She concluded that whoever set them up wanted to kill both of them. She had no idea why.

Michael told Anya about the address found in Tom's Moscow hotel room. She said her supervisor mentioned the address, but that was not the first time she heard that same address. "It was my sixteenth birthday," she said. "My father told me about the time he and Uncle Tom were in the Lubyanka district. He was not certain about when, but really clear about the district. He said that he and Tom had a secret and that the secret had an address. The address was Struska Street 16-25, the same address your people found in my uncle's room."

Michael asked her if she knew anything more about the address. She said that she had not thought about the address for years but after her supervisor mentioned it in preparation for this evening's meeting, she did some research and found out that Struska Street 16-25 is the address of a tea shop.

"I guess I am going to buy some tea," Michael said.

"You mean, 'we' are going to buy some tea," she corrected him.

"No, Anya. We have to be careful. Remember I 'hired' you for companionship for this evening. How do we explain anything further?"

"That is easy, Mr. Clark," she said playfully. This is Moscow and I am a special, let me say, service. It is not unusual to 'engage' such a service for more than an evening. If we are seen together throughout your visit, it will not raise suspicion. We meet each day and go about our date," she said with a shy smile.

"Anya these people, whoever they may be, are extremely dangerous."

"They killed my father. I may be an analyst and spend most of my day in front of a computer, but I have been trained to protect myself and I can handle a firearm. Besides, I was informed that your Russian is terrible. You will need me to translate. You need my help," she said, and she was right. He only had a few days and having someone who understands the city and who could bridge the language, will make every minute count. Michael accepted the added complexity of having this young woman as part of the assignment.

## Chapter 7

Michael, wearing a dark blue suit, red tie and black overcoat, arrived at the Moscow headquarters of Enerprov early the next morning. Enerprov occupies the top twenty floors, forty-one through sixty, of one of Moscow's tallest towers. He was there to meet with Pavel Invanov, Senior Vice President and Head of Corporate Security. Michael was cleared by the security guards in the lobby and took the elevator to the fifty-first floor reception area. The mature woman behind the reception desk was attractive and poised. She stood up, walked around the desk, politely asked for Michael's coat and put in on a wooden hanger and hung his coat in a side closet. He was a few minutes early, as he likes to be, and was asked to take a seat and someone would be out to help him shortly.

Michael thanked her and turned from the reception desk toward the seating area. He stopped for a moment to look out at the city from one of the large glass windows that surrounded the reception area. He observed a modern city coming to life on a clear cold winter morning.

His mood was broken when he heard a strong voice call, "Mr. Clark. How nice to see you. Please excuse what is not the best English, but I am understood, yes?" asked Pavel extending his hand and continued with, "I am Pavel," said a big man with a vice-like grip.

"Please, call me Mike."

"I will. I like that, Mike. Come out to the elevator, we are going up to sixtieth floor to meet Mr. Chekhov. He is pleased that you have come and wants to say hello to you," Pavel explained.

The two men took the elevator to the sixtieth floor, walked through a smoked glass door, which Pavel buzzed open with his security card. They walked into a large room that was the waiting room to Andrei Chekhov's office. One side of the room was a wall of windows. The three other walls were clad with white marble, broken only by the smoked glass entrance door on one end and a large beautifully finished dark wooden door that lead to Andrei's private office, on the other end. All of the room's furnishings, including a beautiful couch and three high back chairs surrounding a large glass coffee table, were antiques.

Across from the sitting area was a small brass desk with a beveled plate glass top. The desk was empty except for a flat panel monitor, keyboard and mouse. Behind the desk, standing in front of a period appropriate comfortable looking chair, was a tall stunning blond haired woman in her forties. She was wearing thin black framed glasses, a tailored red suit with skirt and the latest in high heels. Her glasses shielded incredible green eyes. She smiled at Michael, who thought to himself, "Are all the women in Moscow gorgeous?"

The woman walked around her desk, offered her hand to Michael and with prefect English she said, "Welcome Mr. Clark. I am Sasha, Mr. Chekhov's assistant. He is expecting you, please go in." She gestured with her free hand to that beautifully finished wooden door to Andrei's office. She reached for the polished brass handle and opened the door.

In Russian, Sasha announced Michael and Pavel to Andrei, as they all walked through the doorway. The office, like the outside room, was meticulously decorated with antiques. Sasha left the men and walked out of the office, closing the door behind her. Andrei, wearing a white long sleeve shirt and bright blue patterned tie, walked over to Michael and the two men shook hands. Michael, finding himself standing with Pavel on his left and Andrei in front of him clutching his hand, observed that in addition to gorgeous women Moscow seemed to be populated by large males with strong hands.

"It is nice of you visit my country and my company," Andrei said. "May I call you, Mike? Mr. Clark is too formal and the wrong way to address a friend," he added.

"Please do, Mr. Chekhov, oh, I'm sorry, Andrei."

Both men laughed and Andrei said, "Good, now we can build a friendship. On to business, this is an important transaction for Enerprov and we want to assure America that we will be an excellent corporate citizen. I am sure that Pavel will make you feel extremely comfortable with all our security protocols. I think you will agree that safety begins with security. Too many people stop with a review of safety records, ignoring the security protocols that are necessary to ensure a safe operating environment."

"I do agree and I am looking forward to reviewing those protocols, Andrei. By the way, I have to thank you so much for the incredible suite at the Kebur Palace Hotel. It is a spectacular hotel."

"My pleasure. You have everything you need, yes?"

"Everything. Thank you."

"Sit, sit, spend a few minutes with me," Andrei gestured and the three men sat down in comfortable chairs that ringed a stone coffee table across from a large mahogany desk. The office was filled with heavy furniture and original artwork on rich dark wooden, raised panel wainscoted walls. The wall behind the desk was comprised of twelve foot high windows, floor to ceiling, running the wall's entire width. But the office was remarkably comfortable despite its large size and opulence.

"I understand that you were Special Forces, Mike."

"Yes sir, 5$^{th}$ Group."

"Airborne?"

"Yes sir."

"How many times have you jumped, if you don't mind me asking?"

"No, I don't mind at all. In training, deployment or combat?"

"Now I am impressed. What is the difference between deployment and combat?

"Well, a deployment jump is fancy way of getting off the bus. Combat, usually means dodging bullets. I made over a dozen of those."

"Pavel here was a Major in the old Soviet Army. He too has experience, like you said, dodging bullets!"

The three men continued to discuss Michael's and Pavel's military experience for a few minutes before returning to business. A short time later, Michael and Pavel left Andrei and returned to the fifty-first floor.

Michael settled in with Pavel and his senior staff, discussing Enerprov security protocols for hours. They enjoyed a light working lunch that was brought in and continued their conversations well into the afternoon. Pavel excused himself late in the day to go back to Andrei's office. He asked Michael to continue reviewing the protocols with his senior staff.

"How is the review going?" Andrei asked, just as Pavel entered his office.

"Good. Mr. Clark is an expert. We tested him a few times and he nailed every challenge. I think he may be able to contribute some original thinking as well. We are saving that for tomorrow. I will make sure that he is given everything he asks for as well as what we want to be sure he sees. The plan is to complete the on-site review by tomorrow afternoon. Mr. Clark said that he would spend Friday working in his hotel room to complete his report, and then he intends to enjoy the weekend in Moscow. I will make sure that he has my mobile number and let him know that he may call me with any last minute questions while he is in Moscow."

"So, what did your man find out about the girl?" Andrei asked.

"He met the young woman at the hotel. They had dinner. She appears to be an escort, just for companionship. She walked back to the hotel with him. She kissed him on each cheek, left the hotel and then went directly to the Metro. My man observed nothing unusual. A young woman companion for some friendly conversation is all that he observed. No problem at all. Mr. Clark travels often and has been to our country before. My man thinks she is exactly what she appears to be; some friendly companionship but, well, no sex."

"Let's hope for Mike that there is some sex," Andrei said and both men laughed hard. Andrei added, "You can end the surveillance. I am comfortable with Mr. Clark. I am sure he will be impressed with our protocols and report the facts. On a personal note, there seems to be more to this American but nothing that I sense is important to Enerprov. Please make sure Mr. Clark has all he needs and insist that he call on us to provide him with anything that will make his weekend in Moscow more enjoyable." Andrei concluded. Pavel has no idea about Viktor's grand plan. Pavel knows of Rushad Umarov, who does work in his division, but only sees Rushad as a special envoy between the Chechnya operation and Moscow. All of Rushad's face-to-face time is with Andrei, not Pavel.

The sun was setting in Moscow, but it was the middle of the morning in Washington D.C. It was a warm day for winter, and people were taking a little extra time walking to their meetings among the many magnificent office buildings that are characteristic of the nation's capital. Inside the large Rayburn Building, Room H-232, the suite of the Speaker of the House, it was all business.

The outer office reception area was busy with staff members speaking on every available phone. In the conference room, additional staff members were also working the land lines and mobile phones. It was a full-court press. The focus was the scheduled vote on the new energy bill. The Speaker had his neck on the line and was making sure that his entire majority knew it. He wanted all their votes in addition to as many votes from the minority party as possible. This bill had to show dramatic bi-partisanship, even if that overwhelming show of cooperation had to be borrowed, bought or threatened. Hence, it was another ordinary day in the office of Speaker of the House, James Harris.

James was behind closed doors, alone in his office. He sat at his desk, located to the left of the American flag that stood at attention in the corner of the office. In his hands, James held the old leather bound notebook. He brought the notebook with him from his home in the posh Capitol Hill residential area. He had not looked at the notebook for more than a year until about a month ago and lately, he needed to have it close to him on a daily basis.

He turned to the notes made that night in November of 1978. He read them carefully, smiled and reflected on how he and Viktor had actually shaped their entire lives based on the wild strategy they envisioned that night after drinking for hours. Over the years, their plans were refined and now they were about to become a reality. He knew what was coming and he knew there was no way to abort. "Would it still work in today's world?" he thought. "Yes it would," he concluded.

The Speaker's thoughts turned to Andrei. "Could Andrei carry on for Viktor? He was raised for this purpose as the singular driving force in his life," he thought. Viktor chose his son because he wanted to be sure his life's work would be achieved if anything happened to him. Viktor told no one else.

The Speaker never shared the plans or the notebook with his wife or his two sons. No, his family would not have to deal with this and if anything happened to him, then so be it. Not Viktor. Viktor made sure that at least one other generation would try. What started with Viktor and James was now up to Andrei and James. The Speaker closed the cover of the notebook and starred into the quiet of his empty office reflecting on his long friendship with Viktor Chekhov, while the rest of suite was filled with people engulfed in high pressure conversations.

Chapter 8

After two full days at Enerprov's offices, meeting with Pavel and his senior staff, Michael was happy to have the solitude of his hotel room. It was Friday morning and his intention was to compile his findings into a report for Bricksen Grove. It took Michael a few hours to complete his work and e-mail it to New York. His suite at the Kebur Palace Hotel had a comfortable desk at which Michael worked on his report. The hotel also had an excellent high speed wireless Internet connection but Michael used his mobile phone as a secure, encrypted "hotspot" to connect to New York. This was standard procedure for any normal Bricksen Grove security engagement. Michael was born into the Cold War and grew to adulthood considering the Russians as enemies, so being in Moscow this procedure seemed even more appropriate.

With the cover engagement completed, Michael remembered he had Anya's mobile number from the text she sent him on Tuesday night. He sent her a message asking, "How are you? Meet me in the lobby at 4:00 p.m.? I thought we could go for tea. I hear there is a great little shop in Lubyanka," he joked in his text message.

A few minutes later, his phone buzzed, "I would love some tea. I will see you in the lobby at 4:00 p.m.," she replied.

Michael, wearing slacks, a dress shirt without a tie and a sport coat was sitting in the hotel lobby with his coat folded and draped over the arm of his chair. He was reading an English version of the local paper and wondered if the translation was completely accurate. Some old Cold War biases are hard to change. He looked up from the paper and saw Anya hurrying through the front entrance, her long black hair trailing in her wake as she moved swiftly and gracefully. Her coat was opened revealing that she was wearing a neat white blouse and black slacks with two inch black pumps. "I wonder if my Cindy would have been as confident as Anya. I know she would have been as beautiful. God I miss her. I miss Sharon," he thought to himself, as he stood up to greet Anya.

She moved directly to him, putting one arm around his back and kissed him on each cheek. He returned the gesture with the same European kiss to each cheek.

"I am ready for tea," Anya said. She suggested that they use the Metro. Michael agreed, grabbed his coat and they left the hotel. The train came within a few minutes and the ride to Lubyanka took only an additional ten minutes. They surfaced onto the street just as the late afternoon sun was starting to set, but still bright enough to keep the air the warmest it had been in days. Coats were still necessary, but opened, not buttoned.

"Struska Street 16-25 is this way," Anya gestured. They crossed a busy avenue and walked three streets to Struska Street and began to look for numbers. The oversized sign for the small doorway that is 16-25 was clearly printed in Russian with a simple message, "Tea for You." It was a nice personal touch for a large cosmopolitan city.

Michael and Anya walked into the tiny shop, a clean but dimly lighted space. They found themselves in a narrow walkway between two tall display cases that ran the length of the shop. Each display case has a glass front through which a number of different lose teas, sold by weight, are visible. Behind each case is just enough room for the merchant to walk and open the rear sliding doors of the case in order to access the teas. A small counter at the end of the case to the customer's left (upon entry) is equipped with a modern scale and digital cash register. The modern devices are clearly out of place with everything else in the shop and a reminder of today's electronic age.

"What are we looking for?" Anya whispered to Michael.

"Think about the shop and why your uncle would leave a note with its address," Michael replied.

"Uncle Tom hated tea. He never drank tea that I remember," she said "My father was a different story. He loved tea and my uncle would always make fun of him. There was one tea in particular, a peach blend, which Uncle Tom would always bring my father whenever my uncle was in Moscow. This must be where he would buy it," she said and paused as she remembered something. "Wait! My father told me that in his early years with the old KGB he used to use a tea shop to pass messages to other agents. This must be the same shop. I bet my uncle knew this too. Their secret wasn't the existence of the shop. It was using the shop to pass messages. That was their secret and my uncle has obviously has used that method to pass something to me. That must be why he left the address to be found, but I still don't know what we are looking for," she said.

"Who, not what, Anya," Michael said. He pointed to the shop's owner, a short, frail man of about eighty years of age, who slowly walked from a small room in the back of the shop to where Michael and Anya were standing. The shop owner made some remarks in Russian.

Anya translated for Michael, "He says hello and welcome. He asks if you are American." In Russian, Anya told the shop owner that Michael is an American.

"Ask him if he sees many Americans in the shop." Anya translated, asking the question. The shop owner paused before answering and then replied in Russian. Anya was startled by what he said.

"I did pick up some of what he said," Michael told Anya and continued with, "I thought I heard him say "not since last week or something like that?"

"He said much more. He said that he has something for me and that he recognized me from a photograph. He said he had not had an American customer since last week and he said that particular customer showed him a picture of me. He said the American told him that I might come by and that if I did he was to give me a package." She asked the shop owner for the package. Before he gave it to her, he asked her to describe the American who had her photograph and what was the nature of their relationship. Anya, assuming it had to be her uncle, described Tom Moore and said without hesitation that he was her uncle.

The shop owner smiled. He walked slowly into the back room and was gone for a few minutes. He returned with a box of packed tea. He put the box into a bag, folded the top of the bag tightly and handed it to Anya. He said in Russian, "This is from your American uncle, some wonderful peach tea. He asked me to tell you that he loves you very much."

The shop owner smiled again, said there was no charge and returned to the back room. Michael and

Anya could see him sitting down and picking up a book. Apparently, their visit was over.

"Let's not open it here," Michael said. I suggest we go someplace quiet, someplace other than the hotel," he added.

"My apartment is only twenty minutes from here by Metro."

They left the shop and after a brief wait and exactly twenty minutes on the Metro, they walked three streets to a small apartment building. They went inside and up a flight of stairs to Anya's one bedroom apartment. The front door opened into a square hall just to the left of a small modern galley kitchen. Her apartment was neat, organized and decorated tastefully but without frills. It was furnished as many young professional Russian women like with enough features for comfort and efficient living, but easy on the budget.

Anya removed her coat and took Michael's. She tossed both coats on her couch in the single large room that serves as both a living room and dining area. The dining area was furnished with a charming small round wooden table, surrounded by four straight back matching wooden chairs. She placed the bag from the tea shop on the table and gestured for Michael to sit, while she pulled out a chair and sat down herself. Both sat still for a moment looking at the bag.

"Anya, please open the bag," Michael asked quietly. She opened the bag and removed the small white tea box. She hesitated for a moment and opened the box, which was filled with loose peach tea, its pleasant aroma quickly filling the air. Her expression indicated that she did not understand. What possible message was the box of tea? Then Michael, reaching for the box said, "May I?"

Anya nodded and Michael took the box and tuned in upside down, spilling all the tea and a key on to the table.

Michael picked up the key. "There are no markings on it" Michael observed. "Have you ever seen a key like this?" he asked her. Anya did not say a word as she gently took the key from Michael's hand. She immediately recognized it and stood up and ran into the bedroom, retuning with a wooden box about the size of a book.

She sat down again placing the wooden box on the table. The box was made of cherry, light in color with a figure of a magnificent horse beautifully carved into the top. The box was easily over seventy years old and its two brass hinges and brass keyway were pitted with age. "My father gave me this box when I was a little girl. It was quite old at that time. I was only eight years old," she said. Anya fought back a tear before she continued, "My mother passed away that day after a two year battle with breast cancer. He knew how shaken I was and how little I understood why I would no longer see my mother. He gave me the box and told me a story that went with it. He gave me something tangible to hold on to in order to help me, such a young child at that time, cope with the grief."

"Do you know what is in the box?" Michael asked.

"No. The story my father told me was simple. He said that the box contained secrets that needed to be protected and asked me to protect those secrets. He asked me to only open the box after I grew up and graduated from university," she paused and gently moved a hand over the carving of the horse. She continued, "He said that the horse belonged to a handsome prince and that if I protect the box, the prince would appear and protect me if I was ever in danger. It was the best story a little girl could hear. Protecting the box gave me something to focus on at that time. As I grew up, the box was always a grounding point I would come back to for help in strengthening my discipline and resolve. My father was truly brilliant."

"The key opens the box?" Michael asked.

"It is the key my father gave me when he gave me the box, but I never opened the box. Even after I graduated from university, I still did not open the box. I did not want the fairytale to end," Anya said as she could not hold back her emotions any longer and her eyes swelled with tears. She fought as hard as she could but the tears were stronger and started falling from her now reddened eyes.

Michael took her hand from the box, pulled her into his arms and hugged her. Anya did not resist. She welcomed the comfort and allowed her tears to fall more freely. All her grief for her mother, her father and her uncle was too much to ignore. Her tears penetrated Michael's heart as he felt her grief combined with the grief he carries for the loss of Sharon and Cindy.

In a few seconds, she pulled back and Michael released her from his embrace. She looked at him and said she was sorry for her unprofessional behavior. Michael smiled and assured her that her reaction was human and perfectly normal. He told her there was nothing unprofessional about it and that he was happy to be a friend to her. She smiled and for the next few seconds nothing was spoken, but much was said.

Anya dried her eyes with a tissue, looked at Michael and asked, "Should I open the box?"

## Chapter 9

CIA headquarters in Langley, Virginia was in crisis mode this Friday morning. Reports were intensifying about increasingly active chatter on various Internet sites used to pass messages among suspected terrorists around the world. The chatter revealed the possibility of a bombing planned for Washington, D.C., though few in the Agency believed that any group would be bold enough to attempt an act of this kind and even fewer believed it could actually succeed. The chatter was non-stop. Complicating matters was an equal amount of chatter, also pointing to Internet websites as the communications channel, regarding a bomb plot targeting Moscow. Like Langley, the headquarters of the FSB in The Lubyanka Building in Lubyanka Square in Moscow was also in crisis mode. There have been deadly bombings in Moscow in the past and the FSB was taking the situation seriously.

With information coming into Langley and Lubyanka Square at a record pace, the CIA and the FSB called for a rare joint review of all the intelligence. Teams were assembled in their respective situation rooms; rooms equipped with advanced teleconferencing systems and connected via a secure encrypted network.

David Capella was part of the Langley team. He was about to leave his office for the situation room, when his mobile phone chimed the arrival of a text message, "Sorry for the delay; busy with the cover engagement. I made contact with Anya on arrival. She's a cute kid and smart. I am more comfortable now that I met her. She will be here soon and we will be following the lead you gave me. More to come," read the message from Michael. David was happy to see that Michael was handling things in Moscow. For some reason, after reading Michael's text, he sensed that the chatter and the murders might be related. Having an independent in Moscow could prove valuable. He needed to better understand the intelligence, but David's instincts were telling him that perhaps Michael needed to be brought into the loop about the chatter. Was the chatter connected to the execution of Tom Moore and Oleg Petrov, or was it something unrelated. David needed to sort this out before diverting Michael from his current efforts.

Twenty analysts, sitting around a large conference table, were focused on the individual flat panel monitors in front of them. Above the table, on the wall at the far end of the room from the entrance, were three large flat panel monitors. Two of the monitors were alternating displays of maps and tabular data. The third displayed a live feed from the FSB situation room in Lubyanka Square. The rooms were remarkably similar in layout and equipment. Even the people in the rooms appeared to be same. The only real difference between the rooms was that one was CIA and the other one was FSB. David's boss and the Head of the Agency's Counter Terrorism Task Force, John

Henderson, took charge of the Langley team as he entered the room asking for everyone's attention.

John's counterpart at the FSB, Vladimir Grigoriev, took control of the Lubyanka Square team and settled his people so that the meeting could begin. Simultaneous translation was suspended on agreement that it would be more productive to hold the meeting in one language and the session was conducted in English. The meeting lasted for hours. Sharing of intelligence was genuine, which was further proof of the serious concern each organization has about the chatter.

Vladimir had a distinguished military career before joining the Service more than fifteen years ago. He commanded a Soviet special operations unit during the conflict in Afghanistan in the early 1980's. He is a tough man made tougher by war, but he is also a brilliant thinker. His ability to out think the enemy served him well on the battlefield and then in his first years with the Service as a field agent. He was promoted quickly based on all his experience and his ability to think. His mind is well suited to intelligence work and he is known to quickly and accurately approach large amounts of information and strip away the noise to find actionable data. His leadership skills are legendary in the Service. The combination of his physical toughness and his mental agility make Vladimir the perfect person to head the FSB's Counter Terrorism Unit.

John Henderson, unlike Vladimir, was never in the military and was never a field agent. The CIA recruited John while he was a student at the Massachusetts Institute of Technology. When he graduated in 1980, his classmates went off to Boeing, Lockheed, IBM and other major leading corporations, but John moved to Langley and joined the CIA. John's genius is his ability to organize multiple sets of complex data and accurately find hidden patterns of actionable intelligence. He quickly rose through the ranks and was promoted to various management roles where he applied his finely tuned mind across more than one critical situation. John is similar to Vladimir in his leadership ability. His leadership and unique genius combine to make him the Agency's best pick for his current position.

The situation facing both the Russian Federation and the United States required the best of both countries. John, Vladimir and their respective teams are the best. They will figure out if the chatter is real and if it is, they will figure out how to deal with it.

"Vlad, our current analysis keeps pointing to this coming Monday as the target date. We are still working decoding all the details, but Monday is a definite in all the intelligence we have gathered to this point," John said. He added, "Thus far our analysis on the details indicates that the event will involve a bomb and that the bomb will be only part of the event."

"Our work keeps showing Monday as well, my friend." Vladimir responded. "We also believe the event will include a bomb and that there will be more to the event than the bomb. We were able to sift through the chatter further and are reasonably certain that the bombing will be on mass transit and occur during the evening rush hour," Vladimir added. "There is more, John," Vladimir continued. "Our analysts believe that the threats to both cities are connected and that they will be attempted simultaneously. If we are correct, Washington would be targeted for your Monday morning rush hour. Hitting both cities in real time would be a significant victory for these bastards."

"Your analysis helps to fill some of the gaps in our work, which also indicates a simultaneous trigger. I agree that it would be a major victory for the terrorists. I can shed a little light on who these actors may be or to whom they may be connected. While we cannot confirm our findings just yet, we are reasonably certain that the threat is originating in the Chechen Republic. All data keeps pointing to the Chechen Republic."

"This is most interesting. Thank you. I believe your team is correct. Plugging in the data you have provided confirms our own suspicions. I am positive this threat is emanating from the Chechen Republic. We both have more work to do, and I suggest we get our field people to push on their sources and see what they can add to what we are picking up from the chatter."

"That is an excellent suggestion Vlad. I will get on it immediately here in the States," John said. He paused and added, "One other thing Vlad, both our President and Vice President will be in Washington on Monday. The chatter indicated something about national leaders. Please share with me what you know about your President's schedule, it is important?"

Vladimir hesitated out of instinct, but immediately recovered understanding how serious the chatter is and said, "Our President will be in Moscow on Monday. We picked up similar mentions of a national leader. The bombs could be a diversion and we could be dealing with assassination attempts, but we need to be completely sure about this possibility before we ask our Presidents to alter their plans," Vladimir responded.

Without any further speculation and keeping strictly to the known facts, both teams agreed to meet again in twenty-four hours and use the intervening time to clarify current thinking, while field agents try to pull more tactile data from their sources. The large monitors went dark and the Langley team began to scatter to individual stations and listening posts.

"John," called David, as he walked over to his boss. "John, as you know we have an independent in

Moscow right now and he is working with an FSB analyst on the murders. I know it is premature but I sense a connection between the chatter and the murders. If I am right, I think it will help to provide our man with an update about the chatter."

"I have never doubted your instincts, Dave, but this chatter is indicating assassination attempts. We really need to know more because there may be no connection at all. I will call Vladimir and see what he thinks. If he agrees, you can move forward and update your independent," John told David. The two men discussed the chatter for a few minutes before separating.

In Landover, Maryland, a Chechen sleeper cell was organized over six years ago. Its members, four men, came to the United States before they were radicalized through readings and postings over the Internet. They were also recruited into the cell over the Internet. Each man was an integral part of his community and the two with families were typical of most Landover families. The men have professions ranging from automotive technician to medical professional. Each knows of the others, but none of them ever met or directly communicated with the others. The two wives have no idea that their husbands are in a cell and they have no idea of any radicalized thinking. The men successfully isolated their political beliefs and their secret lives from the community and from their families. They communicate only through Internet websites and remain invisible to each other. They are a prefect sleeper cell. This mission would bring them together for the first time. If they lived or died as a result of the mission is not important, only the mission itself is important.

Halil's visitor visa was good for ten days for the primary purpose of attending an energy conference in D.C. for Enerprov. There was nothing unusual about a respected engineer with Enerprov entering the country for a legitimate business purpose. To avoid questions about his travels to Landover, Halil disclosed on his visa application that he had a family member living in that suburban community.

Halil arrived at Washington Dulles International Airport, rented a car, and drove to the Grand Hyatt Hotel in the Capitol District. He checked into the hotel, put his bags in his room, returned to his car and drove to meet Bashir at a local Starbucks in Landover.

Bashir was anxious to meet the leader of his mission and he was excited about being selected to serve on the mission cell. He waited over six years for this. Bashir, with his wife of only three months at the time, came to the United States in 2004 to escape the insurgency following the Second Chechen War. He studied locally in Landover and became a certified physician's assistant. He established himself at a local hospital, where he still works.

Bashir, a devoted Muslim, was slowly radicalized over the Internet and then recruited in 2007 to take a role in the Chechen Separatist movement. He and his wife now have two children, but neither his wife nor the children have any idea of Bashir's involvement with Chechen Separatists.

Over the past several months, Bashir followed the instructions that were hidden throughout various web pages on the Internet. He purchased the staging site, a recently constructed single story home with an attached carport in the center of a bankrupt development. All other homes in the development were only partially constructed and a large undeveloped field was behind it. The site was on edge of town and isolated from the rest of the community. Bashir also accepted the materials that were delivered to the site. He sent keys for the site to specified locations for pick up by the other cell members. A schedule, for tasks to be performed at the site and for which cell member to perform a specific task at a specific time, was also embedded in various web pages on the Internet.

All the cell members would check the schedule for their assignments and the dates and times for them to go to the site to perform their work. They would arrive at different times in order to maintain their anonymity from each other. The coordination and discipline was precise. The cell executed all the preparations and everything at the site was ready for Halil and for the mission.

Halil pulled into the parking lot and recognized Bashir, waiting for him as planned, from a photograph he had seen in Grozny. He parked the car, turned the engine off, left the car and walked over to Bashir's car. Bashir immediately opened the door of his car, got out and stood watching as Halil approached him. "Bashir, my brother," Halil said as he hugged Bashir. They spent a few minutes standing and talking. "I understand that you and the cell have it all together," Halil added.

"Yes, it is all there and all ready. The drones and the missiles arrived in several pieces, but Elbek assembled them perfectly. I am looking forward to meeting him. I read that he is an incredible automotive technician and can assemble anything mechanical. I am also looking forward to meeting the others. They also did all that they were assigned and their work is also done. All of the control equipment is assembled and it tested successfully. The bomb is ready and the lethal gas has been mixed. The canister containing the gas still needs to be attached to the bomb. Also, the missiles need to be fueled and mounted to the drones. Everything is ready according to the instructions we received. We all followed the schedule and never deterred from it."

"Excellent," Halil said. "There is one more delivery coming. It will arrive tomorrow at your home. Do not open the package. Sunday night there will be instructions on the Internet for you to follow on Monday morning. It is important that you follow those instructions and bring the package with you. Everything will be ready on time for Monday morning," Halil instructed him.

"Of course I will do as you say, no problem, I will receive the package and I will check the website for final instructions," Bashir responded

"Good. Does your wife suspect anything?"

"No. She suspects nothing. She is a good Chechen woman. When it is over, regardless of what happens to me, she will be proud and will understand," Bashir told Halil.

"Have you seen all the embedded messages on the Internet verifying that the entire cell is ready and that they know about Sunday?" Halil asked.

"Yes, Halil, the messages were clear and the members have followed all their other instructions perfectly, so I am confident they will do the same with these. They will join you at the site on Sunday for last minute preparations and will remain with you for Monday's mission," Bashir answered.

"You did well, my brother. Allah is smiling. I am sure of that," Halil said. The two men went into the

Starbucks and shared some coffee speaking only about the latest news from Grozny.

In Moscow, Rushad met Mumadi Bassyev. Mumadi, like Bashir in Landover, is a member of a sleeper cell. This cell is in Moscow. Mumadi is also a trained physician assistant. He immigrated to Russia from Chechnya in 2007 and did so as a dedicated Chechen Separatist. He immediately organized the cell using the anonymity of the Internet. By design, the Moscow cell is identical to the Landover cell. The expertise of the members, the isolation of their true intentions from both family and community, the notice of the mission, the mission logistics and the progress report were identical to that in Landover.

Mumadi took care of everything and the staging site was fully prepared. Rushad was pleased. Rushad also told Mumadi about a last minute package and gave him instructions similar to those Halil gave Bashir, to check the website before leaving for the staging site on Monday.

The Moscow bomb will be detonated at 6:30 p.m. on Monday night. Simultaneously at 9:30 a.m. Monday morning, the Washington, D.C. bomb will be exploded. Seconds later, the targets will be eliminated.

Rushad, as a member of Enerprov's security staff, was able to travel in and out of Russia as he needed. He was as also able to help others move in and out of the country, as long as he was careful. Andrei had friends in certain parts of the government, but not in the FSB. The Service, not to mention the Russian Federation President, would love nothing more than to find a legitimate reason to see Andrei in a Russian prison.

"Mumadi, what did you learn about Oleg's daughter?" Rushad asked.

"I had someone follow her for a few days and this past Tuesday they saw her meet an American at the Kebur Palace Hotel. We only know that the American is staying at the hotel as a guest of Enerprov. He is some sort of consultant who was sent here to work with your boss, Pavel, on something that has to do with clearance for a transaction."

"The American must be a security consultant here in connection to Enerprov's offer to purchase U.S. energy assets. News of this potential deal is all over the media. Why else would he need to see Pavel? I am a small player at Enerprov, my friend. They don't include me in much, but that would be my guess. Remember that this company is just my resource. Andrei Chekhov is using me and I am using him. His only goal is power, but he is useful. I put up with him and do as he says. He provides all the funding we need to do what the Chechen people and Allah need us to do," Rushad said. He paused and continued, "But what would Oleg's daughter want with the American?"

"I don't know. Perhaps she met him in the past. I learned nothing that would trouble our mission, certainly not at this point. I did not want her to get suspicious, so I had the person stop following her," Mumadi said.

"You made the right decision. I certainly don't want to risk anything now, but I am troubled about what she might know. We do not have the time to find out if she is a threat, and we can't risk exposure by approaching her. We will have to eliminate her. I still have three members of my strike force in the city. I kept them here just in case we ran into problems. I will have them take care of her. If this American gets in the way, then that will be unfortunate for him," Rushad concluded. He was pleased that the mission was on schedule and he took it upon himself not to risk any problems, real or imagined.

## Chapter 10

"Should I open the box?" Anya asked.

"Anya, it's time. Yes, please open the box," Michael answered. He looked at Anya and realized that though she may be an analyst with the FSB and though she may be trained to be tough as well as smart, she is also a young woman who just had her father taken from her. The box is an important tangible connection to her father and a reminder of how well he took care of her. Opening this box will be a major leap in Anya's life. Once she opens it, she will forever leave behind the innocence of her childhood.

She picked up the key from the table, gently guided it into the keyway and turned. The click was loud and clear. She lifted the brass tab that was just released, clearing it out of the way to open the lid of the box. She slowly ran her hand over the carving of the horse and said to Michael, "You know, I still believe that the prince is real. I know it's foolish, but I need to believe it," she said shyly. "I hope the prince will understand," she added, as she gently lifted the lid and opened the box.

There were few contents in the box, just two folded papers. Anya lifted the top paper and unfolded it to reveal a colorfully printed text on heavy stock. It was the Russian fairy tale *The Scarlet Flower* which told of adventure, daughters, a father's love and even a charming prince. It had everything any little girl would cherish. On the bottom, handwritten in black ink, was a short note in Russian. Anya translated, "My Dear Anya, Someday there will be a charming prince who will win your heart. All my love, Papa (30-3-1997)."

"My mother died on March 30, 1997. My father, I always called him Papa, must have prepared this the same day," she said. She placed the priceless paper down and unfolded the second paper. It was a letter to Anya, handwritten in Russian.

"It is also from my father but it is dated just last month. He must have come to my apartment when I was working. He knew that I kept the box in my night stand by my bed. I remember telling him that I could guard it better at night if it was close to me. I kept it close to my bed growing up and I know that I told him that I continued to do the same in my own home. He must have come in, added the letter and then left with the key."

"There is really little doubt about that, Anya," Michael said. Would you mind reading the note?"

"No, I don't mind," she said and started to translate, reading out loud.

"My Dear Anya," the letter started. She read on, "If you are reading this letter, it is because I am no longer with you. I am so proud of you. No father could ask for any more from a daughter. You gave me so much joy. Your mother would have loved to live to see the beautiful woman you are, but I am sure she is looking down on you and loves you. I was never a religious man, the Party made sure of that. Your mother was a devout Christian and braved the Party. When the Soviet Union collapsed and religious belief was once again embraced in Russia, she was able to practice her Christianity openly. She was much braver than I. When you chose to follow her in her faith I was truly happy and I hope you will always have your faith to comfort you."

Anya continued to read and translate, "I can only imagine how difficult it was for you to open the box. When you decided to leave it unopened on your return from university, I assumed you were going to wait till, well, till I was no longer with you. When I first gave the box to you, as I am sure you figured out by now, it was a gesture to help my young child facing the loss of her mother. I wanted to give you something to focus on and become part of your life. An inadequate replacement for your mother, but still something found for something lost. It is obvious that you protected its contents well and I am so proud of you. Do you remember *The Scarlet Flower*?" Anya paused and told Michael, "This was my favorite story."

She continued reading Oleg's letter, "Your job of protecting the box is complete but there is one more task you need to do for me. The note will explain. Your task, my sweet Anya, is to find the best way to deal with what you are about to read."

Oleg's letter to Anya continued to describe how he was assigned to accompany Viktor Chekhov on November 15, 1978 to meet with an American at a pub one street from the entrance to Lubyanka Station of the Moscow Metro. She stopped reading and thought she should explain to Michael "Last year I reviewed all the FSB and prior KGB history on Viktor Chekhov as part of an assignment on Enerprov. You probably know Viktor's history was that he was a baron of the black market. If it was hard to come by in Soviet Russia: alcohol, clothing, food, machinery or drugs, Viktor would find it, acquire it and sell it. All of which was illegal, but successful enough to buy Party officials low and high in the government." Anya paused, and then said, "The KGB, and then the FSB, hated this man."

Michael was familiar with Viktor Chekhov. He read everything the CIA had on Enerprov, Andrei and Andrei's father, Viktor. Michael understood that Viktor's main focus was the oil and natural gas industry and that he worked his Party connections to obtain private ownership of all the legitimate assets his black market profits could purchase. Michael learned that Viktor was quite successful and that when the Soviet Union collapsed in 1991, Viktor emerged as the sole owner of one of the largest oil and natural gas producers in the country. That company was Enerprov. "I know of

Viktor's history," Michael said to Anya. "Please continue reading your father's letter," he asked her.

The letter went on to tell of the meeting between Viktor and this American. The two were supposed to share a drink and about thirty minutes of conversation. These brief encounters between citizens of rival super powers were routine for the time, but the meeting of these particular citizens was unusual. The KGB did not like Viktor, but the Party protected him. Oleg's letter described the American only as the son of a wealthy influential oil family. Their meeting lasted hours but there was no record of the meeting or the identity of the American.

Oleg wrote that the American was accompanied by a CIA agent. That agent was Tom Moore. Oleg and Tom accompanied Viktor and the American into the pub but sat at another table across the room. Tom's Russian was excellent and Oleg was fluent in English. The two agents got to know each other by alternating their conversation between English and Russian. Oleg explained how by the end of the evening the two agents found out that they had more in common than they had differences. Oleg added that they both understood that while in another setting they might be compelled by duty to kill each other, they still could be friends. His sense of humor was dry and always present.

Feeling comfortable with Tom after a few hours, Oleg wrote that he asked Tom about the American. Tom was honest, primarily because it really did not matter, and said he was only told about the importance of his family and to refer to him as Citizen X. Oleg said that over the years, he and Tom had stopped talking about the meeting and stopped trying to figure out the identity of the American.

Oleg wrote that he observed Viktor and the American exchanging gifts at the beginning of the meeting. The American reached into his jacket and pulled out two elegant pens. He handed one to Viktor and kept the other for himself. Then Viktor reached into his coat, which he had placed on an empty chair by the table, and took out two, leather bound notebooks. He gave one to the American and kept the other for himself. It was at that point that Oleg became curious.

This was an unusual exchange of gifts. It appeared to have been arranged beforehand, Oleg explained, because the two men kept writing in the notebooks throughout their conversation. Oleg explained he was so curious about the exchange that he pointed it out to Tom, who had already noticed it himself.

By the end of the evening, especially when the meeting lasted for hours, Oleg confessed to his new friend that the bartender was KGB and was supposed to photograph Viktor and the American. According to the letter, Tom laughed so hard and tried equally as hard to conceal his laugh, that he almost chocked himself on his beer.

Oleg's letter continued from there with, "The photograph was lost for decades, until I found it only a few days before I wrote his note. Many of the old KGB files were scrubbed before its reemergence as the Federal Security Service. I had an opportunity to review some of my old KGB files and I found the photograph. Your box, my daughter, your mysterious wooden box has a false bottom. Push against each end in the opposite direction and you will find the photograph. The photograph is faded. It was not stored properly, which was no surprise considering all the internal problems at the KGB during the transition to today's Service. However, the American's face is clear enough and could help identify him. Find out who he was. Find one of the notebooks, Viktor's or the American's, and I am sure you will discover what there was about that original meeting that is important today," Oleg's perception was keen.

His note continued, "I apologize for entering your home unannounced, but I knew you would eventually open the box. I have been haunted by the meeting in 1978 and recently I had the sense that I needed to try once more to find out the truth. I also sense that I am in danger, so that is why I took these steps. Perhaps this is just the paranoia of a field agent at the end of his career. I intend to send the key to your

Uncle Tom. Since you are reading this note, either your uncle brought you the key or he returned to your home. I know that you will discover the truth. All my love forever, Papa"

Anya and Michael looked at each other. She lifted the box and opened its false bottom as Oleg instructed. Inside was a nine centimeter by nine centimeter square, black and white photograph. It was grainy and faded, but the face of the American was somewhat clear.

"I think it is time for me to check in with the Service," Michael said to Anya.

"I agree," she answered. "Let's go now, back to the Lubyanka District and to the Lubyanka Building, where the Service is headquartered. That is where I work," she added. Anya carefully closed the false bottom to the box and neatly folded both the printed nursery rhyme and her father's letter. She placed both, along with the photograph, into the main compartment of the box and closed the lid. Instinctively, she locked the box. She reached for her large purse on the chair next to her, and gently put the box and the key in the purse. She took a deep breath and successfully fought back another tear.

By now, the growing darkness of the evening began to set in. Anya started to reach for the wall switch to turn on the overhead light so it would be easier to find their coats, when Michael gently took her hand and stopped her. He put his finger to his mouth and motioned for her to be quiet. Michael had been sitting with a full view of street through the apartment's front window in his line of sight. He noticed a car pull up after it approached slowly, as if searching for a building number. He observed three men in long overcoats exit the car with military efficiency. Michael sensed danger and was not going to take any chances. He whispered to Anya, "Stay quiet. Do you have a gun in the apartment?' he asked.

"I don't. I know how to use a gun, but as an analyst I am not assigned one," she answered quietly.

"No worries, we'll improvise," Michael assured her. A minute later he heard movement in the hallway outside of her door. He remembered how narrow the hallway was, so only one man at a time would be able to approach the door. The others would be immediately behind him, most likely in a row.

In the hallway, the men acted exactly the way Michael assumed. Each man reached inside his coat and removed a heavy semi-automatic Bulgarian made Arcus pistol. Each pistol had a suppressor screwed into the front of its barrel. The men showed no emotion. They were here to kill, to kill quickly and then leave.

Michael gestured to Anya to lie down on the floor at the back of the living room and she did as he asked. He then quietly walked to the front door, stopped opposite from the side it would swing open and stood there motionlessly. The sun had gone and Anya's apartment was in total darkness. Michael's heart momentarily raced but he took a deep breath and quieted it down. Positioned at the door, with all his senses on full alert, he waited completely still for what seemed like forever. He was so perfectly calm that one could reasonable wonder if he had a pulse.

Suddenly with the sound of breaking wood, the door flew open as the man on the other side kicked it hard and entered. Just as Michael hoped he would, the man entered with his gun drawn and charged. Michael quickly put both of his hands around the attacker's double hand grasp of the gun's handgrip. Michael turned the man's entire body 180 degrees, aiming the gun at the second man in line, just as the first attacker pulled the trigger of the semi-automatic pistol. The sound of the shot was muted by the suppressor, as the bullet found it mark landing between the second attacker's eyes.

Before the third man could react, Michael squeezed the first attacker's fingers against the gun's trigger and fired a second round and then a third. Both bullets hit the third man's chest and he fell to the floor dead.

Michael, still in complete control of the first attacker, twisted the gun free and smashed its handgrip into the man's face. The sound of breaking cartilage accompanied by spewing blood confirmed the broken nose, but that would not be enough to stop this man. The attacker fell against door jam, pulled a serrated combat knife from its sheath in his coat and lunged at Michael holding the knife low to come up into his target's midsection. There was no time for anything other than reflexes and instinct. Michael's main priority was Anya's and his survival. Without any hesitation, Michael simultaneously deflected the lunging knife with one hand and fired a fourth shot from the assailant's gun at close range into the man's head. It made a terrible mess against the wall.

"Anya get the box and its contents, our coats and let's get out of here now," Michael shouted. He carefully unscrewed the warm suppressor from gun and put it in his jacket pocket and tucked the gun in his waistband. Anya stood up, grabbed her purse and scooped up their coats. Michael reached out and took her hand as she followed him out of the apartment, stepping over the three dead assailants. She did all she could not to get sick. Anya was with the FSB for three years following university and her only field assignment was in her capacity as an analyst on surveillance behind a conference room wall in the posh Moscow Ritz Carlton. She received combat training but never saw anyone shot and certainly never saw anyone killed in front her.

Two dead men outside her apartment, another one actually in her doorway, along with all the blood and human matter sprayed everywhere was all she could absorb. The fact that these men were here to take her life pushed her emotions into overload. But she kept her focus and dealt with it. Who is this American who came into her life only days ago? Is he real? He just stepped between her and death. Now her hand is in his and he is pulling her over bloody bodies. Combined with the emotional strain of opening the box and reading her dead father's letter; all that just happened would have left any other young woman completely catatonic. Not Anya. She is Oleg Petrov's daughter.

They ran into the Metro and found a train waiting. Twenty minutes later they were back in the Lubyanka District and quickly walked the few streets to Lubyanka Square and into The Lubyanka Building and FSB headquarters. They approached the large chest high marble security desk, behind which stood two security agents on duty.

Anya showed her credentials and asked Michael to hand his passport to one of the security agents, which he did. Michael noticed the metal detectors they would be walking through, and he mustered up his best Russian to tell the security agent that he had a gun and was going to hand it to him unloaded. The agent instinctively tensed and placed his hand on his holstered weapon and alerted the agent next to him. He told Michael, in Russian, to proceed. Michael understood and slowly removed the Arcus from his waist band and ejected the magazine, catching it in his free hand. He handed the magazine to the second agent and then pulled the slide of Arcus as he turned the gun sideways for the chambered round to harmlessly fall onto the security desk. The security agent let the cartridge roll on to the floor, keeping his eyes carefully on the American. Michael slowly handed him the unloaded gun to the first agent and stood still.

Anya, at Michael's request, told the agents that Michael needed to reach into his jacket pocket to get the suppressor. They nodded their permission and Michael proceeded to hand over the remaining piece of Bulgarian hardware. The agents both looked at the gun, the magazine, the cartridge on the floor and now the suppressor and then they looked at Anya. The expression in their eyes spoke perfect English as if to say, "Really?"

In Russian, Anya asked the first agent to call upstairs, that this is an emergency and to please clear her American friend. She said that the FSB knows who he is and that her department will confirm it.

After the call, the security agent said to Anya in Russian that he would have the gun brought upstairs. Michael was handed a visitor's badge and cleared to accompany her. They took the elevator to the fourth floor where she works and went directly to her supervisor's office. She was relieved to see that Alexander, a tall thin man with short gray hair and a neatly trimmed beard, also quite gray, was still in his office. His thick glasses gave him the look of a university professor and his plaid sport coat enhanced the image. Alexander is a career inside analyst. He is a brilliant man who has solved many difficult analytical problems for the Service, but he would hardly survive more than a few seconds in the field.

"Alexander," Anya called to him as she and Michael approached his small, internal, windowless office. She continued, "We have a problem. This is Michael Clark. He is the American management consultant," she paused and then said, "You will recognize him as the person sent by the CIA to assist us in the investigation of my father's murder."

Michael extended his hand to Alexander, who immediately recognized him from the file provided by David Capella's office. For his part, Michael assumed that Alexander would be connected to the case since as Anya's supervisor he would have approved her involvement in the investigation. Michael told Alexander about what just transpired at Anya's apartment, which genuinely startled the supervisor. He interrupted Michael saying to Anya, "This is why I did not want you involved in the investigation. You still have much to learn. I know Oleg was your father Anya, but these are horrible people we are dealing with," He said calmly and then looked at Michael and continued, "We assigned her to work with you against my better judgment. Thank you for protecting her, Mr. Clark," he said.

Alexander asked for a moment while he used the phone on his desk to call Internal Security and asked them to immediately send a team to Anya's apartment. If the police had not arrived, the team will be able to clean up the scene and secure Anya's apartment. If the police are there, the FSB will take jurisdiction. He also asked Internal Security for permission to place Anya in an FSB protected location until the matter was resolved.

Completing the call, he turned again to Anya and asked, "Are you okay, Anya? I am sorry if I embarrassed you, but we lost your father and I do not want to lose you," he added. "The Service has a place where you will stay for the next few days. Make a list and I will have people get what you need from your apartment," he said to her.

"I am shaken, but I am okay," she said, almost convincing herself. "Thank you for helping me," she continued and said she was not embarrassed and appreciated his and the Service's concern. She showed Alexander the letter and the photograph. He agreed with Oleg's comment that, from what he knows of the KGB history, these meetings between Soviet and American citizens were not documented. He was also not surprised to see a photograph.

"These notebooks would make interesting reading," Alexander said.

"It is obvious that what happened tonight, this letter, the 1978 meeting and the execution of Oleg and Tom are all related," Michael said. "The first step to reaching at least one of the notebooks is to identify who is the American in the photograph. Would you have it scanned and sent to my handler, Dave Capella in Langley?" he asked.

Alexander took the photograph and walked across the floor to have it scanned and sent electronically to David Capella's office. Michael used his secure mobile phone and sent a text message to David, briefly explaining what happened and alerting him to the photograph that was on the way.

Alexander returned and he, Michael and Anya continued to discuss everything that was known about Enerprov, Andrei Chekhov, Viktor, Oleg and Tom. The fact that events were separated by thirty-six years was a real mystery. Then Anya, reading from a file on Viktor Chekhov that Alexander shared during their discussion, said "Monday, January 27th, this coming Monday would have been Viktor's seventy-fifth birthday," she said assertively and continued, "I remember some transcription I did last year on a surveillance assignment, listening to some Enerprov telephone calls. One particular call was from Andrei to a mobile number we triangulated on and found the recipient of the call was in the Chechen Republic. Enerprov employs over three hundred people in Grozny, so none of us thought much about a call to a mobile number in the Chechen

Republic. However it was what Andrei said on the call that made little sense then but may actually mean something now. Andrei said that Viktor would be pleased with Andrei's present in honor of his seventy-fifth birthday." Alexander's facial expressions revealed to Michael that Anya's remarks triggered something that Alexander was not telling them. At that point, Alexander's office phone rang.

"Yes," Alexander said answering the phone. "David, how are you. Yes, he is sitting right in front of me and Anya Petrova is with us as well. I will put you on speaker," he added.

"Michael, this is Dave," the voice over the speaker announced. It was David Capella calling over the shared encrypted link that the CIA maintains with the FSB. The call was transferred to Alexander's office. "Let me also say hello to you, Anya. It is a pleasure to meet you. I am so sorry about your father. I understand that he was a good man," David said. He took a breath and continued, "Together we will find out what happened to your father and our agent. Michael, the American in the photograph has been identified. Alexander, I have permission to share this with the Service, but it is highly sensitive," he said and paused.

"I understand, Dave. The Service accepts responsibility," Alexander responded. David needed to share the information under the terms of their cooperative agreement but wanted the formality of having its sensitivity recognized.

"The American in the photograph is James Harris," David said.

Michael's reaction was immediate, as he stood up and said, "Speaker Harris?"

"I am afraid so, we have a number of photographic images of Harris from his younger days. In fact we have images of him throughout his life. There is no doubt Mike. The American in that photograph is the current United States Speaker of the House. It took our facial recognition software only seconds to get several hits." David added.

Michael, seeing the confusion on the faces of both Anya and Alexander, took over the call. He provided some more detail about Oleg's note, the Tea Shop, the key, the wooden box and the attack on Anya's apartment. He also told David about Anya's observation about Viktor Chekhov's seventy-fifth birthday this coming Monday and also about the comment from Andrei regarding a present in honor of his father's birthday. He asked David if he had any information that could bind all of this together and connect it to the murder of Oleg and Tom. He looked directly at Alexander, remembering his facial reaction to hearing the date of Viktor's birthday.

"Alex, it is time to share with Michael. The Agency agrees and Vlad gave his okay, as I am sure he told you earlier," David said, "Anya as well if it okay with the FSB?"

"Yes. Vladimir explained it to me, and I agree. Yes, Anya can hear as well," Alexander answered.

"The Agency and the Service independently picked up extensive chatter of planned attacks scheduled to take place in Moscow and Washington this coming Monday. We have our situation room in Langley in full crisis mode and Alex will tell you that the Service is at the same level of alert in Lubyanka," David said. Alexander nodded affirmatively. It was Friday evening and the potential attacks were less than seventy-two hours away.

Chapter 11

More than two hours passed and Rushad heard nothing from his hit squad. They used a car stolen from outside the city. They left their mobile phones and all their personal identification in a safe place a distance from the target, but surely they would have returned and retrieved all that by now. He had them time their attack to the time Anya usually gets home from work, based on what was learned of her routine when she was followed for a few days.

What troubled Rushad more was that there were no reports anywhere in the news media about a shooting in a Moscow district that is popular with young professionals. There was nothing on television, radio or the Internet. Nothing. Either they killed her quietly in her apartment and were delayed getting back to their mobile phones, or the FSB has taken control of the scene and blacked out all news. If the FSB is there, it does not mean the squad was not successful. But why has he not heard from them? He had to find out.

The staging site in Reutov is a small rundown two story house, located adjacent to an abandoned Soviet era industrial plant in a relatively deserted part of the city. The prosperous business district is only a short walk downtown, but it might as well be on the other side of the world. The site's location, a seldom visited part of the city, is the perfect place for the cell to remain hidden until it is time to launch the attack. Rushad arrived at the site a few days ago and has been staying there.

It is only a short drive from Reutov's business district to Anya's apartment in Moscow, and Rushad decided to walk downtown and hire a taxi to take him by her apartment. He needed to see for himself what had happened to his squad of mercenaries. About fifteen minutes later, he arrived in the more populated and still bustling business district, found a taxi and told the driver the address to Anya's apartment building. He instructed the driver to drive slowly past the address and not stop. He said he was checking up on his girlfriend and wanted to see if a rival lover's car was nearby. The driver smiled and drove off.

The taxi reached Anya's building in less than forty minutes. There was a single police car parked in front of the building, but there were also three distinctive black UAZ Hunters. The SUV's were obvious FSB vehicles. Rushad noticed five young business types gathered by the entrance to a small park that was across the street and only a short distance from the building. All of the young people were looking intently at Anya's building. Rushad ordered the driver to pull up and stop by the group.

Rushad put his window down and asked the group in general, "You all look as though you saw something where the police car is parked. I am a freelance Internet blogger. Can you share with me anything I could write about?"

One of the group, a twenty-something woman dressed in a long coat that hung perfectly above the ground by exactly the height of her distinctive heels, said, "We saw a number of police cars pull up to the building but then those SUV's showed up and all but one police car immediately drove away."

A thirtyish man in a neat gray business suit and an opened blue overcoat said, "There was a police van parked in front of the building earlier with other police cars. As soon as the SUV's showed up, several men in plain clothes entered the building with the uniformed police officers from the van. Minutes later, the uniformed officers came out of the building carrying what looked like a covered body and placed that body into the van. The officers went back into the building twice more. Each time they carried out what looked like another body and placed it into the van. The officers then got into the front of the van and drove away," he said. "I walked over to the building to see more and was told by a man in plain clothes that I should not get any closer. He said the situation was a Federation matter, and I should mind my own business," he added.

Rushad smiled at the young people, put his window back up and instructed the driver to take him back to Reutov. This was a problem on many levels. Those three men were the only security for the cell and it would be impossible to bring in any additional support at this point without getting noticed. While it would take days to figure out the identity of the dead men, the FSB would eventually tie them back to Chechnya. It is obvious to Rushad that Anya did not stop his squad. "Could it have been the American? He must have been with her. That is the only explanation. But who is he?" Rushad thought to himself.

Rushad has no choice but to go forward with the mission. He took it upon himself to eliminate Anya and he failed. He was not about to tell Andrei. There was no reason for Andrei to know about the attempt on Anya's life and certainly no reason for him to tell Andrei that it did not succeed. Andrei could do nothing about it anyway. Rushad was singularly focused on the mission and would concentrate all his energy on mobilizing the cell for success. If the American, or Anya, gets in the way, Rushad would take care of matters himself.

At the Lubyanka Building, two members of FSB Internal Security walked into Alexander's office. The two had a no-nonsense presence about them. One was a man of average build in a suit and the other a woman, also of average build and wearing a suit with slacks. They asked Anya to go with them to be debriefed on all that happened. They would take her to an FSB safe house and they would stay with her. "I want to remain on the investigation," Anya protested.

"You will," Alexander said and continued, "I promise. Please go with these two agents for now and I will call you personally as soon as we find out more," he assured her. She reluctantly agreed but believed that Alexander would keep his word. She walked to Michael and put her arms around him and hugged him so tightly that he had to search for a breath. "Thank you, Mr. Clark, thank you," she whispered into his ear, kissed him on each cheek and left with the agents.

"Mr. Clark, would you like to see our situation room?" Alexander asked. "We don't often provide tours to CIA, let alone their independent contractors, but having saved Anya's life, the life of one of our analysts, you are now family. Welcome to the FSB," he added.

Michael walked into the FSB situation room, which was occupied by a full team of twenty analysts with eyes glued to flat panel computer monitors. There was a constant buzz of conversation in the room, unfortunately for Michael it was all in Russian. He was managing to pick up a few words, and he clearly was able to discern the seriousness of the mood. They were all racing the clock to save lives. Alexander brought Michael over to meet Vladimir, who was clearly in charge.

"Vladimir, this is Mr. Michael Clark, Michael, this is Vladimir Grigoriev," Alexander said. Michael offered his hand to Vladimir, who took his hand but then immediately pulled Michael into a full body hug and said in English, "Thank you for protecting our Anya. If Alexander has not told you, you are now family. You and me, we are brothers," he said as he released Michael from the hug. "John Henderson, my counterpart in Langley, says that David Capella thinks you are one of the CIA's greatest assets but that you are not regular CIA. He says you work for hire, from time to time, on specific assignments. I am impressed. I understand that you were Army Special Forces. I see that you have not lost a step."

"Thank you. Dave makes more of me than I am. My usual assignments are boring and uneventful. Most often, I am handed a package and I'm gone. That's the truth."

"Yes, we have 'interceptors' as well. Sometimes it is better to have an independent arrive at the end of a mission, intercept the package by design or by force, and then fade away," Vladimir said. "Sometimes because of circumstance, they, as you did earlier, have to get more involved. You all are brave and capable. Regardless of the motive, country or money, you all seem to be effective," he added. "I hold you 'part-timers' in high regard. It is not easy to inject yourself into an unknown situation and be prepared for whatever may come. I think you all would make ideal full-time agents," Vladimir said.

Alexander took a few minutes to update Vladimir on all he learned. They spoke in Russian as Alexander showed Vladimir Oleg's letter, the box and the photograph. Michael stood patiently, hearing his name mentioned several times.

Alexander finished his update and Vladimir turned to Michael and in English said, "We have a puzzle and one that may be connected with what we could be facing here in Moscow and your people could be facing in Washington. We just completed a link with Langley and will connect again in about twenty hours. I think it would be good for you to join us at this location for that session," Vladimir strongly suggested to Michael.

"I will be here," Michael answered. He asked, "This chatter? Does the FSB think Enerprov or Andrei Chekhov himself is involved?"

"Yes and yes. We are sure of it. But the company and Andrei have many friends up and down the Federation bureaucracy and it is impossible to nail anything to the company or to Andrei. The good news is that our President hated Viktor," Vladimir said, paused and then continued, "He has developed an even greater hatred for the son. We will have all the help we need from government when the time is right."

"The notebooks Oleg described in his letter to Anya. Have you heard of such a notebook in Andrei's possession?" Michael asked both Alexander and Vladimir.

"Something that personal would be at Andrei's primary home in the Ostozhenka District, here in Moscow. Trying to get into that apartment would be close to impossible," Alexander offered. Vladimir agreed.

"Okay, then we will have to try through Speaker Harris. I will call Dave and see if my side could help," Michael said. He asked if he could use an office and was shown a small private conference room where he could make his call.

"I promise the room is not bugged," laughed Vladimir and then added, "Now, if we were still KGB, the bug would have bugs. Oh, I assume the Arcus pistol which you gave to our surprised security agents is not yours?" Vladimir asked, smiling and continued, "My guess is that you don't want it back?"

Michael appreciated the joking because it was starting to set into his mind that he had just taken three human lives. He killed while in theater in the army and he had to use force a number of times while contracting for the CIA, but this was the first time since Desert Storm that he purposely and ruthlessly took a life. He knew it was necessary. He even separated his own survival from the equation and rationalized that killing the attackers was necessary to protect Cindy. "Cindy?" he thought to himself. Did he really react so brutally because he thought he was protecting his daughter? "Anya! Her name is Anya! She is not Cindy!" he said to himself, as he realized that he would never be free of the rage burning within him.

Michael composed himself and sat down by the small round modern conference table. The table top was glass and the stand was polished stainless steel. The room was sterile of any artwork. It was efficient and nothing more.

Michael called David, who answered on the first ring. "Hey Mike. I'm worried about you," David said. "Are you okay? In all the years we worked together, and in those occasional situations like at Heathrow where you had to get tough, I can't remember you having to kill someone. It is never easy regardless of the circumstances, so please let me now if you want to come off this assignment and come home?" he asked.

"I'm okay. Thank you for the option, but I want to see this through. In combat I was always ready to do what had to be done, and I knew that there may be those times on assignment for the agency when circumstances would require me to get physical. I had that happen at Heathrow. But I never thought I would kill again and I never thought it would be as easy as it was. I didn't even think, I just reacted and did what was necessary to protect Anya and myself," Michael said. He paused "I'm really okay," he assured David.

Michael and David discussed the situation at Anya's apartment, Enerprov, the Chekhov family history, James Harris and the chatter about the potential events in Moscow and Washington. Michael asked if there was any intelligence regarding Speaker Harris and his visit with Viktor in 1978. He asked if there was any intelligence about a notebook and its potential whereabouts.

David had no answers, but promised to dig deeper over the next twenty-four hours. If there was a connection between all that happened in Moscow, and in Reutov, with Speaker Harris, David would do his best to find it.

"Do you need anything Michael?" David asked.

"A Glock 17, ammo and three magazines," was Michael's immediate answer. He added, "A Fairbairn-Sykes fighting knife, razor edge and eight inches in length. Also, a collapsible baton would complete the set. I found it quite useful last assignment. Michael had regained his composure. He stopped thinking about the three thugs he just sent to hell from God's good earth and began to think about helping to save lives.

"I will arrange a drop," David assured. "Look for my text," he added and continued with, "Try to get some sleep tonight. It may be all you get for the next few days."

Michael thanked David and ended the call. He walked back to Alexander's office and saw the time was approaching 11:00 p.m. Alexander, now with his jacket off, waved Michael to come inside. "I have a car and driver waiting in front of the building to bring you back to your hotel. The driver's name is Ivan. He is an experienced field agent and he will be available to you for the remainder of your visit," Alexander said.

"After he drops you off, he will make sure everything is secure before he goes home. Other FSB agents are already in place at the hotel and will remain there for the rest of your time with us. Ivan will be back when you need him," Alexander explained as he handed Michael a mobile phone and said, "This is a local phone. All you have to do is press this security symbol," Alexander said, pointing to a closed pad lock graphic on the touch screen of the phone. "Ivan will answer. His English is excellent, unlike your Russian. I don't know what frightened the security agents at the desk more: you, an American, walking into FSB Headquarters and announcing you had a gun; or your tortured attempt with the Russian language," Alexander said and both men enjoyed a good laugh.

Back in the lobby, the same two security agents accepted the visitor's badge from Michael with a smile, but watched him closely as he left the building. Ivan, a tall thin man whose Ichabod Crane stature was exaggerated by the long black overcoat he was wearing, was standing by a large black UAZ Hunter. "Good evening Mr. Clark," he said in perfect English with a welcoming expression, which forced Michael to think about his own lack of language skill. "I am looking forward to helping you, Sir," he added as he opened a rear, curbside passenger door of the four-door SUV.

Michael, sat down in the back seat, thanked Ivan and said he was happy to meet him. He added how appreciative he was of all the help the FSB is providing.

"No, Mr. Clark. Thank you. You saved an FSB life. You are family now and we take that seriously," Ivan said. He closed Michael's door, walked around the vehicle and sat behind the steering wheel, started the engine and drove off for the Kebur Palace Hotel.

Chapter 12

It was 3:00 p.m. in the afternoon in Washington, D.C. and commuter traffic for a Friday in January was moving faster than usual on the Beltway surrounding the city. But this light traffic volume would last only another hour before the familiar endless line of high-end automobiles clog the road for hours of the usual stop and go shuffle. Pedestrian movement through the core of the government complex was busy and purposeful, no different than any other day. The inner-city was its normal mix of struggle and surrender, an unfortunate contrast to the opulence of the richest nation on earth's federal government. All this wealth was so close to the despair of the inner city, in its direct sight, but light-years out of reach. Rich, poor, powerful and meager in and around this city were thinking about the weekend. Chechen Separatism was not an issue on anyone's mind this evening, but that may be the only issue of importance by late Monday morning.

Dave Capella called everyone he knew at Langley. He wanted to see all that was available about Speaker of the House Harris' relationship with the deceased Russian billionaire, Viktor Chekhov. He learned about the obvious political favors that big money always enjoys, and he learned about the hidden personal favors that only true friendship could attain. Speaker Harris and Viktor Chekhov were close, but nothing about their relationship was unethical or criminal and certainly nothing that came close to treason. They were friends, political allies and business partners.

James Harris grew up in his family's oil business in Oklahoma, one of the United States' leading independent exploration and production companies. By the time James was thirty, in 1976, and having been in the family business for eight years following college, he decided that politics was in his blood. He ran for the House in 1980, won his first election and has been part of the political class ever since. He was elected Speaker four years ago, and many say he may be the most influential Speaker in history.

James met Denise, the debutante daughter of Oklahoma's most prominent banking family. She had poise, money, connections and a way of capturing all of the attention in a room. They married in 1979 and have two sons who are now adults. James and Denise Harris are considered Washington's most powerful couple, quite the achievement when you have to compete with that other couple who live at 1600 Pennsylvania Avenue.

James, since his entry into politics, avoided direct contact with the family business which is run by his brother Bill. However he always found legitimate ways of using his political position to add to the family fortune. At first he was satisfied with just having the advantage of easy money. But it was not long before monetary greed gave way to his lust for power. He grew to enjoy the rush of having things done by simply using his position to get accomplished what he wanted.

Viktor Chekhov's life was quite different from James's life. He was seven years older than James and one hundred years tougher. Viktor grew up poor. He was the son of a miner, who died when Viktor was a teenager. Being the oldest of seven children, Viktor left school and took to the Soviet black market to provide for his mother and his siblings. The black market fit him as though it were a second skin. He flourished in everything from petty theft, to the sale of hard to find goods in Soviet Russia. Over time, Viktor expanded into prostitution, drugs and questionable business deals that always seem to have come to Viktor on extraordinarily favorable terms. His desire to accumulate oil and natural gas assets became legendary. He married and had four children, the oldest being Andrei. Viktor was fiercely loyal to his wife and family, even though he was no more than a gangster.

When the Soviet Union finally collapsed in 1991, Viktor emerged with a collection of oil and natural gas assets that were the envy of all legitimate companies across the globe. Those assets formed the foundation of Enerprov, which quickly became Viktor's second love after his family.

Viktor and James's first public appearance together was in 1994 in Washington. Viktor was honored for his contributions to global health issues, a favorite priority of his wife. A few years before that appearance, and more obvious afterward, James would advocate for Enerprov whenever a push from Washington was necessary to transfer technology from United States corporations to Enerprov. Early access to advanced technology enabled Enerprov to grow quickly, multiplying its proven energy reserves and dramatically increasing its profits and Viktor's personal wealth. Viktor's desire for wealth was driven by his fear of ever being poor again.

David leaned back in his chair in his office and looked at all the files on his desk. It was obvious that Viktor and James had a long relationship, but by Washington standards there was nothing about it that was improper and nothing that connected them to the events of the past few days in Russia. There certainly wasn't anything that connected them to the chatter about Monday. David was about to give up when he noticed one small piece of intelligence in an old folder. It was a photograph of young Congressman Harris taken in 1982. He was photographed in his office, sitting behind his desk. The photograph was nothing special except for the leather bound notebook on the top of the Congressman's desk.

"This is too much of a coincidence," David thought to himself. "The notebook has got to be meaningful because of that 1978 meeting," David concluded. He looked at his watch and realized that the afternoon had slipped into evening. He had been going over these files for hours. He knew that Langley was in full operation twenty-four hours a day. Someone had to be available in the archives at this time and perhaps there was some thread of information somewhere in the archives about the 1978 meeting in Moscow.

After a long frustrating call with the archivists, David conceded that the CIA also had no record of those citizen exchange meetings. He hung up the phone and decided he would call it a night and go home to get some sleep. He gathered all the files on his desk together into a single pile, stood up and walked to get his coat from the hook behind his door. He switched the office lights off and began to head for the elevator when one of the archivists, an older gentleman, approached him. "Mr. Capella," he said. "Mr. Capella, I think I found something that will help you," the older gentlemen said. He handed David another folder.

"Thank you, nice of you to bring this up. May I hold on to it for a few days?" David asked. The archivist agreed and slowly walked away. David sat on the top of a desk in a nearby cubical and opened the file. The contents were few, but interesting.

There were three items in the folder. The first was a hand written note addressed, "To File" and it was from Tom Moore. It was dated November 20, 1978, five days following the meeting between James Harris and a Viktor Chekhov. The body of the note explained that

Tom had a look at the notebook carried by the American identified as Citizen X. It was on the drive back from the meeting. Citizen X had too much to drink and fell asleep in the back seat of the car on the way to the hotel where he was staying, registered under a false name. Tom, who was driving, stopped the car and reached back into sleeping Citizen X's coat pocket and removed the notebook. He only had enough time to read a few pages, and never saw a name, before Citizen X started to wake up. He replaced the notebook, and continued to drive.

The few pages he read had two pieces of information that Tom recorded in his note. First, Tom noted that Viktor and Citizen X had seriously discussed what it would mean if the world's two super powers at the time, 1978, would work together. This seemingly innocent thought was actually quite sinister in that the American and Viktor hinted at forcing the union. He wrote no more about it, other than a date that was agreed upon as the absolutely final date for which this union was to occur. That date was this coming January 27th, Viktor's seventy-fifth birthday. The same date as this coming Monday, the date constantly mentioned in all the chatter picked up by the CIA and the FSB.

The second and third items in the folder were photographs of downtown Grozny. The first photograph was dated 2000, and was taken following the end of formal military action at the conclusion of the Second Chechen War. The downtown was devastated. The second photograph was dated 2011, a few years after the long insurgency had ended and much rebuilding in Grozny had taken place. The devastated building in the center of the 2000 photograph was completely rebuilt in the 2011 photograph and the name on the building, beautifully displayed on its face near the roof in Russian, spelled "Enerprov." The back of each photograph had Tom Moore's signature.

David, realizing that he was not going home yet, walked back to his office, turned on the light, threw his coat on one of his two guest chairs, sat down behind his desk and immediately called John Henderson's mobile number.

## Chapter 13

An important package arrived at the home of Bashir Abramov in Landover, Maryland on a busy Saturday morning for deliveries. This particular shipment was the last in a long and slow stream of materials that Bashir was responsible for accepting and carrying to the staging site. Everything was assembled at the site in a methodical and disciplined order without rush or any sign of anxiety. Patience and discipline are the deadliest weapons of a sleeper cell and this cell used those weapons well.

Bashir watched with the excitement of a child from a first floor front window of his modest two story home as the UPS truck pulled up. He waited until the driver left a tiny package and drove off before he came out of the house through his one car garage. Bashir picked up the package and was curious why it was so small and as weightless as if it was empty. All the other packages arrived by private means, not UPS, and were much larger. He concluded that this must be something special, so he followed orders and left it unopened and put it in his late model European station wagon. He would check the website on Sunday night for final instructions.

The other cell members were also excited that their first mission was about to begin. Each of the other three cell members had their own story and their own specialty. There was Abbas, the forty year old chemist. Abbas worked as a chemistry teacher at the local high school. He was single and lived alone in a one bedroom townhouse. His most critical task was the canister of lethal gas he formulated for the mission. He also had the assignment of mixing the fuel for the missiles, which he had expertly completed. The gas and the fuel were ready and waiting at the staging site. Abbas, a friendly man, was part of a bowling league and considered the 'go to' anchor of his team. He was openly Muslim and did not share the beer, but he didn't preach to his teammates and everyone enjoyed his company. He was a regular guy.

Elbek, at forty-six the oldest member of the cell, is a BMW technician and one of the local dealership's best service professionals. He has been with the same dealership for ten years. His wife of nine years is a nurse for a small medical group. Their seven year old son is a normal suburban boy. Elbek lives on the outer edge of the community in a comfortable ranch style home with a two car garage. Elbek's preparatory tasks for the mission brought him to the staging area many times. He made several trips and spent over two hundred hours fully assembling all the parts into two functioning Russian ZALA 421-12 drones. He followed Halil's designs and modified the drones as planned. Elbek also carefully assembled the missiles.

The drones and the missiles were neatly stowed at the staging site. In his community, Elbek is always happy to lend a hand and help a neighbor with a faulty car or some other household problem. His neighbors say he could fix anything; they say Elbek is a regular guy.

Kerim is a thirty-eight year old electronics engineer who is single and works for an engineering consulting firm in Washington. His job requires him to travel extensively, so he is not that involved in the community. But when he is home during football season he is always happy to open his small semi-attached home to his neighbors for a Sunday afternoon of viewing several NFL games on his large flat panel television. Kerim is a regular guy who drives a twelve year old SAAB four door hatch back and enjoys viewing a good football game with local friends. Like Elbek, he too went to the staging site at his assigned times and found all the electronic parts he needed to fully assemble the equipment to be used to control the navigation of the Russian ZALA 421-12 drones.

Abbas and Elbek had military experience that included combat. Bashir and Kerim had no military experience or training. Aside from those differences, Bashir, Abbas, Elbek and Kerim, were four regular guys from the neighborhood who also happened to be four dedicated Chechen Separatists. Their discipline is unshakeable and their resolve is incredibly strong. They spent years patiently waiting, and waiting, and waiting.

Earlier by time zone that same Saturday morning in Moscow, the package delivered to Mumadi was also tiny. Mumadi thought for sure it was empty, but followed Rushad's orders and did not open it. He put the package in his apartment, since his seven year old LADA Kalina sedan was parked on the street and he did not want to risk the package being stolen. He would check the website for his final instructions hours before the start time.

Each of the other Moscow cell members, like Mumadi, lives a life that allows them to blend into Russian society. Similar to their American based counterparts, they are well liked by neighbors and regarded as ordinary folks. Also like their American counterparts, their specialties include chemistry, mechanics and engineering. They also exercised patience, obedience and discipline. They too had everything ready at their staging site in Reutov.

There is a major difference between the members of the Moscow cell and the members of American cell. Just as Rushad is a brutal man while Halil is gentle and cerebral, the Moscow cell members had much more combat experience in the military then did the American cell members. Mumadi was trained as a medic and served, but never saw any action. The other three members of the Moscow cell saw more blood and inhumanity than any person should witness. Their hatred for Russia, though not as intense as Rushad's, was as real and as personal. These were tough men who could be counted on to do anything that would advance the mission.

Two sleeper cells planted in their respective locations years ago, with none of their members having any direct knowledge or contact with the other members of their respective cell. The objective of the sleeper cell is not to attract attention by standing out too much, but also not to raise suspicion by remaining too distant from neighbors. The sleeper cell needs to be a good member of the community and as ordinary as possible. Each cell would come together in twenty-four hours to form a functional team for the simultaneous execution of their respective missions in Moscow and Washington.

Michael woke up early on Saturday morning, in his comfortable bed in the elegant Moscow Kebur Palace Hotel. He started his day with a long workout in the hotel's well-equipped fitness center. Michael, mindful that at fifty-six years of age preparation was the key to successful work-outs, spent several minutes stretching and doing extensive core work to strengthen his midsection and lower back. He shifted attention to the weight machines and free weights for the next half an hour. Building muscle when he was in his twenties was a matter of breathing, but now it required concentrated lifting. He finished off the workout with forty minutes on the treadmill at a 7:30 per mile pace and followed that with another round of stretching.

After he showered back in his room, Michael was starting to get dressed to go and enjoy some breakfast in the hotel's restaurant. He was interrupted when his mobile phone rang. He sighed and answered saying, "This is Mike."

"Good Morning Mike, Dave here," said the caller, David Capella.

"Dave, it is 9:00 a.m. on a Saturday morning here in Moscow!" Michael said. He continued with, "That means it is midnight in Langley! Is everything okay?"

"No, nothing is okay. Actually I would have called sooner, but I wanted you to get some sleep after all you went through yesterday. I have news. The archivists found a file that Tom Moore had tucked away. He originally opened the file in 1978 with notes he made from that meeting between Chekhov and Harris. The KGB may have photographed them, but Tom did one better and scalped Harris' notebook after he momentarily passed out drunk in the back seat of Tom's car. Tom had enough time to read a few pages before he had to put the notebook back. He was not able to identify Harris from what he read, but there is some usable intelligence in Tom's note. First, Chekhov and Harris envisioned a union between the Soviet Union and the United States. Second, they agreed that a union of this nature would not occur without some persuasion. They would work to make the union happen and if by a certain date their plans had not come together, then they would take action to force the union. The date they selected is this coming Monday, Chekhov's seventy-fifth birthday.

There's more. Tom updated the folder twice, once in 2000 and once again in 2011. Each time he put a photograph of downtown Grozny in the folder. The significance of the photographs is that when taken together they show the emergence of Enerprov in Grozny."

"So you are saying that the chatter is real and that Chechen's are involved? You also are saying that Enerprov is most likely involved?" Michael asked.

"Exactly, Mike," David said and added, "Since we found this intelligence, we spent the past few hours going over visas, new citizens, student movements everything we could get our hands on relative to Chechens coming into and leaving the United States. We also alerted our friends in the FSB and they have been doing the same relative to Russia. We have found hundreds of leads in the States and are now working feverishly to narrow them to potential suspects."

Michael thanked David for the information, suggested that David get some sleep so he would have a clear mind for the link between the CIA and FSB situation rooms that was scheduled for later that day. There wasn't much more Michael could do until the link. He finished getting dressed in gray slacks and a light blue button down collared shirt, no tie, and dark blue sport coat. He left his room and headed down to the lobby and the restaurant.

When he got to the restaurant's reception area an attractive mature woman dressed in a red blouse, black skirt and modest heels, greeted him and directed him to a small table by one of the room's large windows. Michael sat down and was quickly approached by various service staff members offering coffee, tea and juice. He chose green tea and orange juice. In a few minutes, his official waiter, a short good looking young man, offered Michael an English language menu, as was customary in this international hotel. Michael ordered a simple breakfast of whole grain cereal and fruit. He enjoyed his breakfast as he viewed the city slowly coming to life late in the morning, as is typical for a Saturday in Moscow.

After breakfast and on his way back to his room, Michael noticed Ivan waiting for him by the restaurant's reception area.

"Ivan. Good Morning," Michael said.

"Good Morning, Mr. Clark. I know you did not call for me, but the Service asked me to stay by your side. Your people called us about the information they uncovered and our analysts went to work immediately to follow up on our end. I can also tell you that the bodies of the hostels involved in the murder of agents Petrov and Moore showed up in two different morgues in

Reutov. Our comrades did not go quietly; we found eleven bodies. All eleven, and the three who attacked you and Anya, are Chechen," he said. Ivan's facial expression changed from vague to concern. He continued, "The Service is sure that these thugs are connected to what we are hearing in chatter. The Service is equally sure that their leader is really pissed at you right now."

Michael laughed at this young proper Russian agent using American slang as if it were elegant speech. "Well Ivan, I am equally pissed at their leader," Michael responded to lighten the conversation and both men shared a laugh.

Michael asked if Ivan had knowledge of how Anya was doing. Ivan said he would check. The two men went up to Michael's room, where Ivan waited while Michael brushed his teeth, grabbed a small brief case and his coat. Michael's mobile phone buzzed the arrival of text message that read, "Your package is ready. You may pick it up inside the lobby of the museum, a short walk from the hotel. It will find you." Michael read the message and said to Ivan, "I need to make a stop this morning and pick up something."

"Yes, I know Mr. Clark," Ivan said. "We were told about the package and it was we who suggested the museum," Ivan added. Michael smiled and gestured to Ivan to lead the way.

The two men entered the museum, a majestic building only a five minute walk from the hotel. They slowly climbed the front stairs and walked into the museum's expansive first floor lobby. If there were more time Michael would have enjoyed taking in the Moscow history to which this museum was dedicated, but not this visit. An average looking man in a long coat and typical bulky Ushanka hat approached Ivan and Michael. He identified himself as a paid courier and handed Michael a small brown paper wrapped package and walked out of the museum.

"I know a place where you can test that," Ivan suggested with a smile. Michael just shook his head and said, "Let's go."

The drive to the indoor range took less than fifteen minutes. It was in an FSB building, only three stories high. Security at the desk was friendly. They recognized Ivan and expected to see the American. He was cleared and the guards made no request to check his package. Michael and Ivan used the stairs to go down to the first sub floor and walked into the check-in room of an indoor firing range. They walked into a small room with a large wooden table. The table stood directly in front of a large glass wall that separated the check-in room from the twelve-bay firing range visible through the glass.

A small enclosed corridor, with a door at each end, was the way into and out of the range. The design concept was simple and elegant. Only one door would open at a time and must be closed before the other door would open. This design kept the sound of the gun fire contained and separated from the check-in room. Ear protection was required at all times in the range but not in the check-in room. The enclosed corridor provided the sound protection for those in the check-in room.

A muscular man in a short sleeve shirt and cargo slacks, with a holstered MP-443 on his right hip, stood behind the table. He handed both Ivan and Michael each a sealed packet with foam ear plugs. He also handed each of them a pair of goggles and two boxes containing fifty 9 mm Lugar cartridges each. Michael just smiled at the efficiency of his hosts. The man handed them a key for one of the tall lockers just to the left of the enclosed corridor to the range. Michael and Ivan put their coats, jackets and Michael's briefcase in the locker. Michael opened his package, which contained a molded plastic Glock 17 case, a waist band holster, six boxes of fifty 9 mm Lugar cartridges, a collapsible baton and a metal sheath that held a black, eight inch Fairbairn-Sykes fighting knife with a razor edge. He left the extra ammunition, baton and knife in the locker.

With ear and eye protection in place, both men entered the enclosed corridor, waited for the first door to close which released the electronic lock allowing the second door to be opened. Ivan opened the door and he and Michael entered the range. The twelve firing bays were all free with the exception of a lone shooter at the farthest bay from the entrance. Michael followed Ivan and both men walked along the range. Each bay was separated from the adjacent bays with floor to ceiling walls and a shelf. The left side of the a bay wall was equipped with a switch for the bay's individual lighting and electronic controls to send the target trolley down range or to retrieve it to the bay shelf. The range was constructed of gray painted cinder block. Its ceiling was over five meters in height and the range's length was a full twenty-five meters. Across the range's gray painted concrete floor, yellow lines clearly marked off each five meters from the bay shelf. Michael and Ivan stopped at Bay #6.

The range side of the glass wall, separating the range from the check-in room, was four meters behind and parallel to the bays. Against the glass wall were four wooden tables, arranged end to end, that covered the full width of the range. Each table had a stack of targets located to conveniently service three bays. Several boxes of large metal clips, used to secure the targets to the trolleys, were also spread out along the tables.

Michael walked into Bay #6 and placed the molded case on the shelf and removed the Glock 17, void of a magazine, and pulled back the slide locking it in its open position. He checked to be sure there was no cartridge in the chamber and laid the pistol down, open chamber side up facing down range on the bay shelf. Michael turned around and walked back to the tables, placing the case and the three empty magazines down on the table behind Bay #6. He picked up two of the magazines and carried them back to the bay and placed them and the box of fifty 9 mm Lugar cartridges on the bay shelf.

Ivan removed his MP-443 Grach from its holster on his right hip, ejected its magazine, dropping it into his free hand. The gun was not charged so when he locked the slide open, the chamber was clear. He put the magazine and his gun, facing down range, on the shelf next to the Glock. He put his box of fifty 9 mm Lugar next to the Grach.

Michael proceeded to load seventeen rounds into each of the two Glock magazines on the bay shelf. He walked back to the tables and picked up a target and two clips. He handed them to Ivan. "Please go first. I insist," Michael said.

Ivan switched the bay's light on, after taking the target and clips from Michael. He clipped the target to the trolley and used the electronic controls to send it fifteen meters down range. Ivan picked up his MP-443 and the magazine, pushing the magazine into the handle and charged the Grach by releasing the locked slide. He switched off its ambidextrous safety and, assuming a two hand grip, began to fire. He fired ten rounds in a steady two round per second rhythm, grouping all his shots within three centimeters of the target's bull's eye.

Ivan smiled at Michael, used the controls to return the trolley back to the shelf and removed the target. He then walked back to the table and retrieved a fresh target. He handed the new target to Michael and stepped back. Michael walked into the bay and clipped the target to the trolley. He sent the trolley back down range to the fifteen meter mark. "I will fire some rounds first to get used to the weapon," Michael said to Ivan. "I will try to place them in the outer-most circle of the target," he added.

Michael picked up the first magazine, pushed it into the handle of the Glock, and released the locked slide to charge the weapon. Michael also used a two hand grip, but fired slowly and deliberately to get a feel for the gun. He placed all seventeen rounds in or near the outer ring of the target. Michael ejected the empty magazine into his free hand and placed it and the Glock, with its slide locked open, which the weapon does following the firing of the last round in the magazine, on the bay shelf, turned to look at Ivan and said, "Okay, now let's see if this old American can still shoot." Ivan, standing with his arms folded, smiled.

Michael took the second loaded magazine and pushed it into the handle of the Glock. He released the slide, and maintaining a two hand grip aimed at the target fifteen meters down range. This time Michael fired in the same two rounds per second rhythm as did Ivan. He emptied the seventeen round magazine, placing all seventeen rounds so close to the center of the bull's eye that the group made a large hole out of where the bull's eye was. Ivan shook his head and extended his hand to Michael for a congratulatory handshake. The old American could clearly handle a gun.

Michael and Ivan each sent another thirty rounds down range and then left. Michael was comfortable with his weapon and Ivan was happy to have such a capable person to whom he was assigned to protect.

## Chapter 14

Speaker Harris sat in one of the two Queen Anne chairs on each side of the majestic marble fireplace that served as the focal point of the spacious and traditionally decorated living room of his Capitol Hill residence. The home is an elegant three story brownstone which carries a value of around $3 million dollars in the current market. Most past Speakers were happy to have a small two-bedroom apartment a reasonable drive from the city, but James Harris' wealth was legendary and the brownstone is only one of the several properties he and his wife own across the country.

This five bedroom landmark, with chef's kitchen and enormous great room marked by its distinctive fourteen-foot ceiling, has been the setting for more than one charitable and social event. Denise Harris, the Speaker's wife, is the bell of D.C. and is always happy to play hostess for a worthy cause. Her standing rule of barring political events at the residence has never been broken, but politics was constantly present at all functions held in their home.

James Harris was holding the notebook in his hand. No matter how he tried to ignore it, he could not put it back in the large safe in the residence's library. He had to hold it, to read it and to even hope that it was not real. He wanted to achieve the result, but not this way. Unfortunately, it was all too real. They mused about it more than thirty-six years ago and then actually planned it as recently as four years ago. Now that it was going to happen, Speaker Harris wasn't as sure about it as he had been. He was starting to have second thoughts. His friend and fellow planner was deceased, but the son was even more determined than the father. A highly combustible mix of greed, ego, dedication and honor was not likely to go unfulfilled.

He could not stop it, even if he did decide to try. He could not warn anyone, because he would certainly and rightfully be accused of treason. No, there was no turning back. The only viable option was to succeed and then to bury the evil in what would be left of his soul.

"Jim, my love," called Denise. Her refined and poised voice was a welcomed distraction. "Do you have a few minutes for me or are you deep in thought about how to advance the work of the People?" she asked amusingly. Denise Harris had no idea of her husband's secret. She knew he was a ruthless politician who had little mercy for his political rivals. She watched and stood by as he trampled opponents and advanced his own or his Party's interests. She supported him as a loving wife and reliable partner for thirty-five years. She was the proper mother to their two sons, and always the gracious Washington hostess. Back home in Oklahoma it was not any different. She would campaign with him, fund raise with him and fight by his side on any issue he chose to champion

They are both life-long members of the Democratic Party, a rarity in Oklahoma. They are more conservative than most of their Party, but also loyal to the Party, which in turn constantly returned the loyalty to the Congressman. Their personal life is a true love story. Despite all his power, wealth and prestige, James Harris never cheated on Denise and she never strayed from him. Theirs was a good marriage; a true love; and a true love affair.

Their two adult sons have thus far avoided politics. Denise always demanded that her son's lives be private and would not let them be used in campaigns. Both were free to determine their own political views and career pursuits, and both chose careers in the energy industry that built the patriarch family wealth.

"For you my dear, the country and the People can wait," the Speaker answered.

"Oh, if that were so," Denise quipped.

She spoke with her husband about a charitable event for which she committed the residence and her service as hostess. The event was to take place two weeks from this coming Monday, but the guest of honor, a rather famous Hollywood personality whose presence would unlock the checkbooks of her tony guests, had a sudden change of plans and asked if the event could take place this coming Monday. Since her guest list was comprised of her inner circle of friends, a forty-eight hour notice would be more than sufficient.

The only problem was that James had arranged for her to join their two sons in Oklahoma for the commemoration of a family named, and funded, dormitory at the University of Oklahoma. "Jim, our boys can handle that without me and I decided that this event is far more needing of my time," She told her husband. She was not asking, as she never did when her mind was made up, she was only informing him of her decision.

The Speaker now has a real conflict. He knows he will be safe in the Capitol Building, but with Denise will be out early to personally handle last minute details the evening's event. It is her normal routine to prepare the residence. She could easily be in harm's way in the morning. He insisted that it was important for her to be in Oklahoma, but she dismissed his attempts, thanked him for understanding and left the room. No discussion, Denise had made up her mind.

James clutched the notebook in his hand. His mind raced. His heart began to beat uncontrollably. He had to figure this out. Anything he did to make sure that Denise was clear of the targeted parts of the city would surely be noticed. Someone would figure it out and tie the attack back to him. Now his mind was in overdrive, dealing with a lethal combination of real concern for his wife and with his own paranoia. He leaned back in the chair with his hands over his eyes, the infamous notebook still in one hand, and he tried his best to not think at all.

The day was moving on in Moscow. Ivan, driving from the range with Michael in the front passenger seat, received a phone call and found out from his supervisor that Anya fell asleep within minutes of settling in at the safe house and did not wake up until only an hour ago. He told Michael that Anya was reported to be feeling fine and that she showed little effect from the traumatic circumstances of the prior day. Her training had obviously helped her. The two agents assigned to protect her were both elite veterans and were keeping a watchful eye on her.

Michael thanked Ivan for the update. He was happy to hear that Anya was doing okay. He thought about how different the situation must have seemed for Anya than it was for himself, how frightened she must have been. His training and experience allowed him to set aside fear and focus on overcoming the attackers. He was also able to quickly recover from the stress, though he did reflect for a minute on the fact that he ended three lives, scum though they were. He assumed that Anya was most likely thinking about how she came within seconds of death and how without him, she would surely have been killed.

Michael should have changed the subject in his mind, but it was too late. He thought about how terrified

Sharon and Cindy must have been when the shooting starting in Rome. Were they killed instantly, or did they beg for their lives? Did they have time to pray? Did eight-year old Cindy even know what was happening? Did Sharon see her daughter die? "NO ENOUGH!" Michael shouted silently to himself. "STOP PLEASE STOP?" he begged himself. His emotions ran from grief to guilt and back to grief.

Ivan, noticing a distant gaze in Michael's eyes had to ask, "Are you okay, Mr. Clark?"

"Sorry Ivan, I was lost in my own mind for a moment. I am fine, really. Thank you for asking," Michael responded. Ivan, having served in the Second Chechen War, recognized the signs of post-traumatic stress and he read the file's notes on Michael's personal history. He was concerned for his American friend, but knew not to probe any further.

The two men decided to have some lunch, and a few Baltikas, the most popular beer in Russia. With all the famous German beers produced in Europe, few people know that the Baltika Brewery is the largest brewery in Eastern Europe and the second largest brewery in all of Europe, second only to the Heineken Brewery in Germany. It was a good lunch!

Andrei thought about Viktor as he paged through father's notebook in his apartment in Ostozhenka. Viktor was brilliant. His original notes from the 1978 meeting with a young James Harris were merely the petty thoughts of two ambitious young men. The notes since were much more focused and plausible. Victor's final entries were made only four years ago, one year before he died. They spelled out the entire January 27th mission in great detail. Andrei made all the entries since his father's death, but Viktor's plans needed little refinement.

Viktor pressured James to keep notes parallel to his own and made sure that James and he signed both notebooks after each new entry. They never signed their notes during the early years. But as their plans became more serious in recent times, Viktor wanted the insurance of having James' signature attesting to the plans. This move was genius. The purpose of the notes had nothing to do with instructing a mission. That could easily be done without the notebooks, but the notes with the signatures following each entry served as a confession. Viktor was always suspect of Harris following through, but he had his notebook and Harris' signatures in it. Likewise, not that he would need it, Harris had the same leverage over Viktor. With Viktor dead and Andrei's signature not in Harris' notebook, but with Harris' signature in Viktor's notebook now in Andrei's possession, the leverage was all in Andrei's favor. Andrei closed his father's notebook, smiled and put the notebook back in his wall safe.

## Chapter 15

The situation room at FSB headquarters came to life at 7:00 p.m. when the link with Langley went live. It was 10:00 a.m. in Langley. Both organizations had their senior analytical teams present and positioned in front of their terminals. Michael took a seat at the far end of the table in the FSB situation room to be respectful of the fact that he is just an independent contractor.

"Good evening to everyone in Moscow, good morning to my team in Langley, we will have a great deal to discuss," said John Henderson. He continued, "Vlad, would you and your team like to kick things off?"

"Yes John, thank you. We have been extremely busy since your people called and shared with us your intelligence indicating possible Chechen Separatist involvement. We can confirm that the execution squad who murdered our agents and the three men sent to Anya Petrova's apartment were all Chechen. We pulled all visas, visa requests and recent permanent relocations involving people from the Chechen Republic. We identified over one hundred and fifty permanent residents who emigrated from Chechnya and settled in Moscow, and within forty kilometers of the city, in just the past year. If we are dealing with a sleeper cell, and we most likely are, then the operatives could have been here much longer. It is like looking for a needle in a haystack and you have no idea what the needle looks like." Vladimir explained.

"Now, starting with your intelligence of a possible connection to Enerprov, we looked at all recorded movements in and out of Russia by their Chechen employees. We found that one man in particular has been quite active. His name is Rushad Umarov. He is a low level security staffer, an envoy, known to be a personal friend to Andrei Chekhov. Andrei aside from being, as you in America might refer to him as, a son of a bitch, has a friendly demeanor with all Enerprov employees. It is the one characteristic where he is different from his father. So at first we did not think much of his friendship with Umarov. This man would come in and out of the country acting as a personal courier for Andrei. But over the past year, his trips became more frequent.

Unfortunately as of last week, we lost all traces of him and his whereabouts are unknown. Our agents are looking for him now and we are searching for all contacts he may have made recently," Vladimir concluded.

"Mr. Umarov appears to be a solid lead. Good work," John said. He proceeded to present the CIA's most recent discoveries. He said, "Using the Enerprov hunch, we found seven Enerprov employees who are all currently in the United States. Interestingly enough while six of them are on the transaction team in Houston working on the oil and natural gas asset deal, the seventh, an engineer named Halil Zakayev, is in Washington," John explained. He added that this is the first time that Halil is in the United States and he is registered to attend a conference in D.C. that begins on Monday.

"Now here is the thing about this Halil fellow," John said. "He indicated on his visa that he has relatives in Landover, Maryland. Our guess is that he will be traveling to Landover and did not want to raise our suspicions if we were monitoring him. He is either a really paranoid engineer or an extremely careful terrorist. Regardless, he listed the relative as a local physician's assistant named Bashir Abramov. Bashir has been in our country for ten years. If Bashir is part of a sleeper cell, the cell is deeply covered. This could be a dead end and Halil could just be an engineer taking advantage of the company's dime to visit some relatives," John said.

One of the assembled FSB analysts handed a note to Vladimir and, after reading it, Vladimir said, "I don't think it is a dead end John. Halil is Rushad Umarov's cousin!" That piece of information started a buzz in both situation rooms.

"That is interesting. I don't see this as a coincidence and Mr. Zakayev is someone we will have to closely follow. He has to be connected to all we are hearing," John responded. "We know that Halil arrived at his hotel in Washington yesterday. He was driving a rental car that he picked up at the airport and he left the hotel for several hours after he checked in. I will have our agents find the car and place a GPS tracker on it. We are not sure where he went yesterday, but we will know where he goes now. I will make sure we keep him under constant surveillance," John said.

He continued, "As is routine in these circumstances when we have identified people matching descriptions related to what we are hearing in chatter, we try to learn more about those people. We found Bashir's address and sent a team to his home early this morning to observe him. That team just called and reported that Bashir received a delivery from United Parcel Service at 9:30 a.m. this morning. Our agents said that a minute after the UPS truck drove away they saw Bashir quickly come out and pick up the small box left by his garage. Bashir put the unopened box in his station wagon. That happened thirty minutes before this link went live. We are now accessing UPS records to see if we can find more deliveries that have already taken place or are scheduled to take place later today in Landover or close by. We are searching by package quantity and size to see if any sort of a pattern emerges. We are obviously looking for any recipient of Russian or Chechen heritage. If that delivery is connected to the chatter, and if there are more deliveries that will arrive today, then we will get lucky and identify more cell members over the next few hours. But this is a long shot," John concluded.

Michael thought to himself how remarkable an agent Tom Moore must have been, "Even from the grave, his observations are helping the joint intelligence effort of the CIA and FSB. In addition to Tom's earlier work, what a major break it was to observe the delivery to Bashir's home. It has to be connected. He immediately put the package in his vehicle because he knows what is in it and he clearly is going to take it some place before he opens it. The CIA has a good chance of gathering some more leads if they can discover additional deliveries, or do they? Why would they use UPS and how can one small box be so essential to a sleeper cell that has been in place for years? Tom Moore's work was solid, but the rest just doesn't smell right," Michael thought. But Michael kept quiet because he was not sure and he figured that tracking other deliveries would not hurt anything.

With the intelligence about the delivery to Bashir, the FSB set in motion a search for deliveries that took place over the past forty-eight hours within a hundred kilometer radius of the center of Moscow. The thinking is that if these deliveries are connected to the chatter, the operatives must have needed to have some final component arrive at the last minute. The FSB was using the exact screening criteria that the CIA set up to narrow the search and hopefully reveal something useful.

"John," started Vladimir and continued, "Have you found any connection or suspicion relative to James Harris, your Speaker of the House?" Before John could answer, another one of Vladimir's analysts walked over and handed him another note. "Please John, your indulgence again," Vladimir said and read this note. He looked up at link cameras and reported, "Well, that did not take long. It appears that the delivery of a small package was made earlier today to a Mumadi Bassyev, a Chechen immigrant living in Moscow. We will have people there within the next thirty minutes to observe Mr. Bassyev and his home. Thank you, John for your patience. About Mr. Harris?"

"Not yet, Vlad, but we are working on that. Speaker Harris and Viktor Chekhov were life-long friends and they did envision a union between our two countries back in 1978 and for some reason, God only knows why, they indicated that Viktor's seventy-fifth birthday was the time limit for that union to occur," John answered.

David Capella excused himself and asked if he could have a moment with John. He leaned over to John and whispered, "John, if you agree, I think I will see if I can question the Speaker. He is in Washington and is always available on Saturday's when he is staying in town. It is part of his long standing practice of making himself available to the public and to other House members and their staffs. With your permission I will call his chief-of-staff, who is a friend of mine and an honest man. I will tell him that I need to address an Agency issue. With all we know, it is probably time for the Director to inform Congress. What do you think?"

"Do it Dave," was John's immediate reply. "I will call the Director. He and I will be prepared to provide an update to Congressional leaders from the House and the Senate. The Speaker will definitely demand the update once you speak with him and you make our concerns official," he said.

He then he turned back to the link, "I am sorry for the pause Vlad, Dave thinks having a guarded conversation with Speaker Harris may be helpful and I agree. The only problem is that once the Speaker knows about the chatter, he will expect the Agency to fully inform Congressional leaders. We have a legal obligation to do so. It was only a matter of time before we had to notify Congress and if Dave could get something from Harris that we could use, the time spent briefing the leaders will be worth it. All our discussions will be classified. Nothing will go public. The Agency will make sure of that."

As John spoke, David left the situation room. John added, "Vlad, can someone on your side get in front of Andrei without raising suspicions?"

"Alexander," Vladimir addressed Alexander sitting to his right, "Do we have any excuse we could use to speak with Andrei?"

"I am uncomfortable with approaching him until we know more. Andrei has many political friends, and if approach him unprepared he could escape any responsibility. I suggest we wait until we could find another approach," Alexander answered. Vladimir agreed. They needed to wait until they had more reason to get in front of Andrei,

With all the intelligence exchanged and tasks set in motion, Vladimir and John agreed to reactivate the link as needed without scheduling an exact time. With that, the link went silent.

Back in his office, David called the mobile number of Henry Madison, Speaker Harris's chief-of-staff. Henry answered after the second ring. David and Henry know and respect each other. Henry, a man in his fifties of average height who could afford to shed a few pounds, has been around Capitol Hill for his entire career. He started as a young staff member in the Senate, worked for the Congressional Budget Office as a manager for several years and, since he is a native Oklahoman, he was recruited by James Harris to join his staff. Henry has worked for Mr. Harris for the past fifteen years and while many in Congress are staffed with young, tireless and ambitious men and women, the truly powerful know they need a strong steady hand to run their office. Henry is that steady hand to James Harris.

David explained the situation to Henry without much detail, but made it clear that the Agency has actionable intelligence of a potential terrorist attack and it is now necessary to inform Congress. Henry agreed to set up a meeting and said the Speaker has a Saturday session planned for 2:00 p.m. this afternoon with some staff members, himself included, to discuss a troubled appropriations bill. The meeting will be in Room H 232, the Speaker's office in the Rayburn Building. He suggested that if David could be at the Speaker's office by 1:30, he will arrange for the Speaker to see him. David agreed and thanked Henry.

Michael left the FSB situation room, walking with Alexander to his office. He told Alexander that perhaps he could help provide a path to Andrei. He suggested that he could speak to Pavel, the Head of Security for Enerprov, and see what he may know about Rushad. Alexander liked the idea, but did not want to raise suspicions at the company and certainly did not want to signal Andrei, if he was involved, that the FSB was interested in Rushad.

Michael told Alexander that Pavel gave him his mobile number and offered to answer questions he might have regarding Enerprov security as part of Michael's Bricksen Grove engagement. He said Pavel gave him a list of security personal as part of Michael's due diligence work for the pending asset purchase. Michael had the list with him in his briefcase and when Rushad's name was mentioned in the link with the CIA, he searched the list and found Rushad's name.

The opening to speak with Pavel was that Rushad was listed as "Special Envoy" and is the only such designation on the list. Michael has a legitimate reason to call and to ask about the designation. Pavel's reaction to the name, even over the phone, could be valuable intelligence. Alexander thought about it. He saw Vladimir walking by and stopped and told him of Michael's suggestion, adding that he agreed it could prove useful. Vladimir also agreed, but since it was now past 8:30 p.m., he asked Michael not to make the call until the morning. He said that it would be less suspicious that way. Michael agreed.

Ivan drove Michael back to the Kebur Palace Hotel and said he would only be a phone call away, otherwise he would see him in the morning. Ivan drove off and Michael, greeted by the welcoming smile of the doorman, entered the hotel. He decided to head directly to the bar for a drink before going up to his room. The bar was in the front of the hotel's restaurant, which was even more elegant at night. It was busy tonight. People tend to eat dinner late in Europe and Russia was no exception. Michael glanced at his wristwatch and saw the time was almost 9:00 p.m.

Michael walked up to the receptionist, the same woman who greeted him for breakfast in the morning, only now she was dressed in a suit with a skirt and her heels were higher. She recognized the American and volunteered, naturally in perfect English, that she works a split shift on Saturday: breakfast and dinner. Michael said it was good to see her at both the start and the end of his day. She enjoyed his kind remark and thanked him for the complement. Michael told her he was going to the bar for a drink and that maybe he would think about a late dinner afterward.

The bar was a little less crowded than the dining area, but still a buzz of people deep in conversation. Michael found three empty stools at end of the bar, put his briefcase and coat on the stool at the bar's corner and sat on the one next to it. He ordered Stolichnaya vodka, just to blend in, straight up.

162

When his drink arrived, he thanked the bar tender and he turned his head to see Sasha, Andrei's tall beautiful assistant, walking into the bar. Sasha was wearing a tight-fitting short dark blue cocktail dress that revealed her stunning figure and shapely legs. Her four inch heels added to the allure. Her long blond hair bounced on her shoulders as she walked into the bar carrying her expensive dark fur coat on her right arm, clutching her small evening bag in her right hand. Without her glasses, her beautiful green eyes were clearly visible. She walked directly to Michael.

"Mr. Clark," Sasha said in English, and added, "Believe it or not, this was actually not planned. May I join you?"

"Please do Sasha," Michael said as he stood up, taking her coat and putting in on top of his. She sat down on the third stool, crossed her legs and look directly into Michael's eyes. She was momentarily distracted by the bartender who asked her, in Russian, if she would like a drink. Replying, also in Russian, she ordered Stolichnaya, straight up. "Let's say I believe you that you being here is totally innocent," Michael quipped. He asked, "So what does bring you here?"

"It is completely innocent. I was supposed to meet a friend, a male friend, who I have been seeing for the past few months. Instead of him showing up, he sends me a stupid text message. Well guess what? It turns out he is married and, as you would say, the bastard got caught! He breaks with me with text message!" she said as her perfect English began to fall apart the more she angered. "You think I am attractive Mr. Clark?" she asked.

Michael wanted to say it was a dumb question, but he controlled himself. Attractive? Dear God she is absolutely gorgeous. He did say, "Sasha you are indeed attractive."

"It is not easy Mr. Clark. I am single at forty-one years of age. Men in Russia want young baby factories. They don't want me. I work all the time and when I do allow myself to be friendly with a man, they all turn out to be married, lustful or just jerks. My latest was no different. I am smart girl," she said as her English broke again. "I am pretty. I have good job," she added. She then picked up the vodka the bar tender had just set down in front of her and put it back in one swallow. Michael was sipping his. She motioned to the bar tender to bring her another, composed herself and with perfect English returning said, "I am sorry Mr. Clark that was uncalled for. Please forgive me?"

"No need to apologize for anything. Well maybe there is one thing? The way you drink vodka compared to the way I drink vodka has completely stripped me of all my manhood." he said. Sasha laughed out loud.

"I needed that Mr. Clark, thank you for making me laugh."

"Happy to help, now please call me Mike and drop the Mr. Clark."

"I like that, Mike." she said. They talked for about fifteen minutes before Sasha asked, "Have you had dinner Mike? I have not and, well, I am starving."

"In fact I have not had dinner either and sharing some good food with a new friend would be nice," he answered.

"It is my treat," Sasha said and continued with, "Actually it is Enerprov's treat. I made all the arrangements for you at the hotel, including the instructions to send all your charges to Enerprov."

Michael asked the bartender to put the bar charge on his dinner check and they left the bar. The receptionist sat them at a quaint table for two. The table was freshly adorned with a clean crisp white table cloth, polished silver, crystal glasses and black linen napkins.

Over a dinner of pan seared salmon and vegetables accompanied by a bottle of French Chardonnay, Sasha freely shared her feelings. She needed to talk and her motives were honest, though she did openly flirt. She would have enjoyed it if Michael made an advance, but naturally he did not. She finally, half amusing and half serious, had to ask, "Mike, I am doing my best to seduce you, subtly, but definitely trying. Am I going to have to be more aggressive?"

"No, you are doing fine and I am absolutely thrilled and honored. However, I dare not tarnish my shining armor by allowing myself to take advantage of the most beautiful woman in Moscow, who unforgivably was made vulnerable for one night by the actions of a fool," he said.

Sasha looked at Michael and thought to herself, "How much would his armor tarnish? Was he kidding? After that little speech I am ready for him to take me right here in the restaurant! Damn it, YES, take advantage of me, NOW!" Her verbal response was more controlled, "Thank you for that wonderful thought." While to herself she kept thinking, "I want him!"

Following dinner, Michael walked her to the hotel entrance and had the doorman hail a waiting taxi. Sasha, wearing her fur coat, threw her arms around Michael and kissed him passionately on the lips. In response he put his arms around her, pulled her close and returned the kiss. For a brief moment they shared the same thought. The taxi pulled up and Michael broke the embrace, leaned forward with his arms dropping to her waist and kissed her gently on each cheek. "Good night Sasha, there will be another time for us. I believe that," he said to her as she let go and she got into the cab.

"Another time. Yes Mike. I will dream of that," she said softly, as he shut the door to the taxi and watched it drive off into the cold Moscow night.

## Chapter 16

David used his credentials to quickly pass through Rayburn Building security. He proceeded to the Speaker's suite and met Henry in the outer office reception area. Except for more casual attire, the activity in the Speaker's suite was not any less on this Saturday afternoon than it was during the week. "Thank you Henry for arranging this," David said. He reached out and shook Henry's hand. He added, "How's Ann?"

"Anything for the Agency," Henry replied. "My lovely wife is fine and she misses you and Carol. We need to get together with both of you soon," He added, referring to David's wife Carol. Henry walked over and knocked on the closed door to the Speaker's private office.

A few seconds later the door opened and there was Speaker Harris, sleeves of his white shirt rolled up to the elbow, no tie, collar opened, khakis and casual shoes. With his best politician's smile, James looked at David and welcomed him. He gestured for David to come into the office and sit on the red leather couch next to a the matching red leather high back chair. James sat in the chair. Henry remained outside and closed the door to give the two men privacy.

"So what is this about, Agent Capella?" asked the Speaker. "I remember you from my days on the Intelligence Committee. As I recall, you are one of the good guys and thank you for your service to our country," James added.

"Mr. Speaker, thank you for seeing me on short notice. I always enjoyed testifying before your committee. You would actually ask important questions. I appreciate your thanks for my service, but it is my pleasure to help protect our nation," David replied.

David explained the reason for his visit, "The Agency started picking up chatter about a possible dual attack on Washington and Moscow planned for this coming Monday. We found out that the Federal Security Service picked up similar chatter. We have been communicating with the FSB and openly sharing intelligence. The Russians are as concerned as we are and concur that the threat is credible. The reason why I asked to see you, Mr. Speaker, is that the chatter and subsequent intelligence raised the possibility of Enerprov involvement. I understand you and Viktor Chekhov were good friends and a strange fact relative to this chatter is that Monday is Viktor Chekhov's birthday," David explained. His eyes were focused squarely on James.

In almost every circumstance and at almost any time, the last person you would want to play poker with was James Harris. His control over his demeanor is legendary and he is usually impossible to read. This time was different. The Speaker's face color completely drained of color and his posture stiffened. David just had the confirmation he came for. All the lies and denial that was about to follow could not 'un' ring the bell that just rang loudly.

"Really?" the Speaker said, with color returning to his face. He continued, "Viktor was indeed a good friend. He had a tough life growing up and he over compensated. He was ruthless, but he built a solid company that employs thousands of people all around the world. Why would a company like that be involved in some scheme to attack Washington and Moscow?"

David looked past the Speaker and saw the old leather bound notebook on the Speaker's desk and quickly refocused his eyes on Speaker Harris. Having the confirmation he was seeking, David played along, "I was hoping that you may be able to shed some light on that very question? The date is interesting, don't you think?"

"Viktor was a complicated man, Agent Capella. The date could be a simple coincidence and nothing more. However if the Agency believes the chatter is credible, Congress needs to be informed and DHS needs to be involved. I will have the chairmen and ranking members of the appropriate House and Senate committees available by 3:00 p.m. for a telephone conference using the current dial-in protocol. Has the Agency briefed the Secretary of the Department of Homeland Security?"

170

"I understand that our Director is doing that at this very minute, Mr. Speaker. I will let my boss know of your order for the 3:00 p.m. call. You can be sure that he will have the Agency's Director on that call and you and the other leaders will be fully informed of all we know."

David and the Speaker stood up, shook hands and David left the office. He said goodbye to Henry and walked out of the suite. The Speaker was a real pro. He did let his guard down for a second, but then quickly took charge and attempted to divert focus by evoking all the appropriate steps the law demands in a situation of this severity. It did not matter, the Speaker was up to his gavel in this plot and David caught that in his initial reaction. David also saw the notebook.

The CIA Director completed his call to the Secretary of the Department of Homeland Security and was exhausted after begging the DHS not to evacuate the city and then flood it with DHS storm troopers. The result of those steps would be a panic more destructive than any bomb could possibly achieve. He was also able to convince the Secretary to leave the situation all under CIA control. The CIA reports directly to the Director of National Intelligence who reports directly to the President of the United States. The CIA will coordinate with the FBI on all necessary domestic security measures. The DHS can focus on its fine work of strip searching grandmothers in search of terrorists at airports. This situation was serious and with little time left, the CIA did not need the help of people with little applicable training and experience.

The 3:00 p.m. call with Congressional leaders was pure politics. Each party member took their turn grandstanding, while the people who are charged with saving lives and keeping the nation safe, the Director and John Henderson, had to endure all the meaningless talk. Fortunately by 4:00 p.m., James and the Leader of the Senate both thanked the Agency and offered all the Congressional cooperation necessary. They also reminded all those on the call that everything they just heard was classified and must be kept confidential. They emphasized that any leaks could cause panic and possibly even benefit those seeking to harm the country.

The Director of the CIA told John that he would personally update the FBI and make sure that John had all the resources he needed to protect the nation.

David, now back at Langley, sat across from John Henderson in John's office. "Tell me about Speaker Harris?" John asked.

"He knows something. I have been one-on-one with Harris before when he chaired the House Intelligence Committee. He was always impossible to read. This time he was so obvious that it was embarrassing," David said. He added, "There is something going on in his head. It was obvious to me that he knows something."

"What do you suggest, short of waterboarding? While that might be the only way to get the truth out of these politicians who violate their oath of office on a daily basis, we are not supposed to do that anymore."

David laughed at John's sarcasm. He became quite serious and said, "I think we need to look at that notebook."

"So the CIA should walk into the office of the Speaker of the House and demand to see his notebook?" John mused. He added, "Seriously, how do you suggest we see that notebook?"

"Once again, there is my friend Henry Madison. I will ask for his help," David said. John warned David to be extremely careful in trying to see the notebook, a cautionary reminder that the veteran agent really did not need.

At the safe house within the inner rings of Moscow, Anya was in her pajamas and sitting in bed. She was reading a book she found on a small table in her bedroom. It was an old Russian romance novel and it was a welcomed diversion from all she had recently been through. The time was late, or early depending on your perspective, with the digital alarm clock by the bed displaying 1:00 a.m. It was Sunday morning and she was bored and ready to be back at work. The Service has been wonderful. They care about her safety and the team with her has been courteous and respectful, but it was time for her to go back to work.

She put the book down and picked up her mobile phone. She sent a text message to Alexander. It read, "Sir, I am ready to come back. Please let me be involved. I am ready." She then paused, smiled, and remembered she had the number to Michael's mobile phone. She sent him a text message reading, "Mr. Clark, I hope you are okay. I am fine, rested and well protected. I hope to see you later today, Anya."

Having finally been able to shut his eyes after a long and multifaceted day, not to mention the past few tempting hours with the sensuous Sasha, the buzzing of an arriving text message brought him back to full alert. "Damn these things!" he said aloud to his empty room. He looked at Anya's text message and calmed down.

Her note was as comforting to him as if she was his own daughter. That was the feeling he was dealing with, but this time he accepted it. His only child, his daughter Cindy was with God. He believed that with all his soul, but it didn't help the grief. Caring about Anya helped the grief.

Michael texted back, "It will be good to see you too. Get some sleep, sweetheart, Mike" and then he put the phone down, closed his eyes and forced himself to take his own advice and get some sleep.

"Get some sleep, sweetheart" was the portion of the text message that Anya focused on. She felt like a little girl and she loved the feeling. Her emotions for Michael were not romantic. They each had it right. Whether it was the recent death of Oleg or how Michael protected her, it didn't matter. She wasn't sure if she saw this man as a father image or if he was the guardian prince to whom the carved horse on the box belonged. It did not matter, she needed someone looking out for her now, so she accepted her feelings willingly. She too then fell asleep.

## Chapter 17

Michael's mobile phone's alarm signaled 6:00 a.m., Sunday morning in Moscow. Having managed about five hours sleep, Michael actually felt refreshed, though his head was still in a wrestling match with last night's vodka and wine. He thought about sleeping more but concluded the fitness center would be better for his hangover.

After another intense workout, including a full hour on the treadmill at his usual 7:30 per mile pace, Michael's body was free of the alcohol's toxins and renewed. His head felt much better as well. Taking a white towel from the top shelf of a black cabinet in the corner of the fitness center, Michael wrapped it around his neck and took a paper cup from the dispenser attached to the sleek modern water cooler. He filled the cup with cold filtered water, drank it all and filled the cup a second time.

Michael looked over the fitness center thinking to himself, "The vodka and wine was a good idea last night, but man it certainly is a regret this morning," he laughed with his next thought, "But not as much of a regret as putting Sasha in that damn cab. She has to be the sexist woman on earth!"

He returned to his room, showered, shaved and dressed in slacks and a long sleeve dress shirt and went to the hotel's surprisingly busy restaurant and enjoyed a light breakfast. The time was 10:00 a.m. and Michael signed the check that the young perky waitress brought to the table. He walked into his room, took his mobile phone from the pocket of his slacks and called the number Pavel gave him.

Pavel answered in Russian on the third ring, "Allo?"

"Good Morning Pavel, this is Mike Clark. I hope I am not disturbing you" Michael attempted in Russian.

"Good Morning Mike," Pavel answered in English and mused, "You are not disturbing me at all, except for your Russian. I appreciate your respectful attempt with our language, but I suggest we continue in English,"

"Thank you Pavel," Michael laughed, "I will be leaving Russia tomorrow night and I was checking my notes. I need clarification on one point, if you don't mind?" Michael asked

"No, I don't mind at all, please go on."

"I was reading the list of security personnel you provided and I see a man by the name of Rushad Umarov with the title, 'Special Envoy.' He is the only one so designated and the list has his location as the Grozny Office. Can you tell me what a special envoy does and why this position is so unique?"

"Rushad Umarov!" Pavel said, "I will be honest with you Mike, and this has nothing to do with our security protocols, but I do not like this man. His position is real. It is sometimes necessary to move physical documents between our locations in Russia and our office in Grozny. We like to maintain possession of those documents, so we use our own courier. Andrei likes this Umarov fellow, so he has the job. I think he is a pig. My young cousin had just married a charming girl and together they were working hard to build a good start for themselves when their innocent lives were cut short in a Moscow bombing by those Chechen animals. Umarov is typical of those terrorists. I don't trust him."

"I am sorry for your loss, Pavel. That is terrible. Innocents seem to carry the brunt of all that is wrong with humankind," he paused and could not help think about Sharon and Cindy. He quickly composed himself and asked, "How often does Rushad come to Russia? I ask so I can better understand this position?"

"Usually about once every other month, sometimes twice, but that is rare."

"I assume he is back in Grozny and out of your sight for a while."

"Actually, he was in Moscow only ten days ago. It was strange because my Grozny staff, those I do trust, could not find any reason for his trip other than he was called directly by Andrei. When that happens, I stay out of it. It is Andrei's company."

"Does that happen often?"

"No, but it does happen."

"That answers my questions, Pavel. My work is now complete and I thank you again for all your help and hospitality. I truly appreciate the wonderful accommodations here at this incredible hotel. I look forward to another visit soon, perhaps after the transaction," Michael offered respectfully.

"You are most welcome my new American friend. You come and visit after the transaction and we will have some good drink and better laughs." Pavel responded as they ended the call.

Michael was sure that Rushad was connected to the chatter, he had to be. Michael called Alexander's mobile number and updated him on the conversation with Pavel. Alexander thanked him and reminded Michael that the FSB is on full alert to find Rushad.

At the Reutov staging site, Rushad was inspecting the work of his Moscow cell. Everything looked ready. When the cell members arrive later today, they will attach the canister of lethal gas to the bomb. The missile will be fueled and mounted to the drone.

They would carefully rehearse the entire operational plan for Monday evening and then, wait. Rushad felt good about the preparations for the mission, but he was also concerned. Too much has gone wrong. He should never have lost as many men as he did eliminating Oleg Petrov and his CIA friend. The three men he sent to kill Oleg's daughter should have accomplished their mission with ease and not have ended up dead themselves. Rushad thought again that the American consultant had to be responsible for stopping them. "Who was this American?" Rushad thought to himself.

Rushad was also concerned about the FSB because he was unsure of what they knew. He did feel somewhat better having seen the posting on the website of the alternative instructions for Bashir in the United States. That meant the CIA took the bait. They will follow Bashir. The CIA most likely shared the Bashir information with the FSB, and the FSB certainly would have successfully traced the delivery to Mumadi by now. The FSB will follow Mumadi on Monday, Rushad was sure of it. Bashir and Mumadi will be martyrs, though they have no idea of their pending sacrifice.

Rushad thought about Oleg's daughter again, and the American consultant. Once the mission is complete, Oleg's daughter will no longer matter. He could forget about her. The American is another story. Rushad wanted to settle things with this man and he was tempted to take care of it now, but he knew he could not put the mission in jeopardy. Rushad was sure that the

FSB is looking for him, so he had to wait. He had to remain at the staging site until the mission began and not take the chance of being spotted by FSB agents. He will find the American and settle the score after the mission succeeds.

Alexander read Anya's text late Sunday morning and called Anya to ask her if she was sure about coming back to work so soon. She assured him that she was ready. Alexander agreed, but insisted that she continue to use the safe house and that the security detail will remain with her until they were comfortable that the threat to her was mitigated. She agreed. He told her he would look forward to seeing her at The Lubyanka Building, at her post, later in the day.

Vladimir was not pleased that the FSB search turned up only a single delivery to a Chechen expatriate in the Moscow area in the past few days. He hoped for much more, but it was still a positive lead and it will have to do. Vladimir was also concerned by the message he received earlier from the CIA, that the Agency also found no other deliveries, on Saturday or the day before, to Chechen or Russian expatriates in and around D.C. The CIA has only Bashir and the GPS tracking device they planted on Halil's rental car. Yesterday's analyses at both spy agencies revealed little additional actionable intelligence. All they have are a few threads from which they need to weave enough cloth to prevent the potential disaster that is rapidly heading toward both countries.

Anya waved to Alexander as she walked past his office. She was casually dressed, as is customary when weekend assignments require round the clock surveillance and related analytical work. The FSB sent people to her apartment for items from her wardrobe and she made a stunning petite picture in her form-fitting dressy blue jeans, two inch heels and red sweater. She had her long black hair pulled back into a ponytail, revealing the innocence of her young beautiful face. "It was hard to imagine how this angel was almost taken a few days ago," Alexander thought to himself as he watched her walk by his office, smile at him and go directly to her cubical and her computer screen. He was happy that she looked sure of herself, but he was ecstatic that she was alive and well. She was Oleg's daughter. She was family.

Michael called for Ivan, who arrived within thirty minutes, and met him in front of the hotel. Michael, again in business casual, jumped into the front passenger seat of the SUV. "Good morning Ivan. I need to make a few stops before we go to the Lubyanka Building," he said. "I want to see the building in Reutov where Oleg and Tom were murdered, but before that, I need to go back to Anya's apartment. I need to make sure I am remembering correctly something I observed," he added.

"No problem, Mr. Clark," Ivan responded and continued with, "What is it you are trying to remember?"

"There was something about the way the attackers approached the door of the apartment. I've been trying to picture it in my mind, but I need to be back at the apartment to help me."

Sunday morning traffic in Moscow is not much more forgiving than weekday mornings, but still better. They reached Anya's apartment in thirty minutes. Ivan found parking directly in front of the building. Michael jumped from the SUV with Ivan immediately behind him. They entered the building and ran up the stairs to the second floor. Michael stopped, looked down the narrow corridor to Anya's apartment. At that point it became clear.

He remembered how he assumed the attackers would have to approach Anya's door in single file. That part was easy, but what helped him surprise the first attacker through the door and quickly eliminate the other two before they could fire at him, was that at the moment the first man kicked open the door, the others were focused on the adjacent apartment doors. Instinctively the other two attackers were securing points of advantage and readying themselves to control the tempo of the assault. They never expected the point of the attack to be turned on them because they assumed that the target in the apartment would be caught by surprise and easily overcome. Hence, their primary focus was preventing interference and securing a clean line of egress. Their tactics were standard military urban assault tactics. All these men had military training.

Having seen enough, Michael asked Ivan to take him to the Building in Reutov where Oleg and Tom were murdered. The drive took almost an hour due to the increasing noontime traffic. They reached the building and parked a short distance from the front entrance. The remnants from the firefight were still fresh. Plywood panels covered the empty space where plate glass was prior to being blasted apart by AK-47 and MP-443 rounds. Inside, the lobby was still a mess of glass, wood, metal and dried blood. The building was closed for a good reason.

Michael slowly walked from the lobby to the first floor suite. It was obvious from all the blood stains that many were shot in this location. He saw the chair and the restraints that once held Tom Moore. He was able to deduce how the scene must have been originally organized and how a planned path of retreat would lead to a backup assault position in the lobby. It was clearly another military style operation. They just underestimated Oleg and Tom. The veteran agents managed to send eleven of their attackers to hell before they lost their own lives.

"So, Mr. Clark, what have we learned?" asked Ivan.

"Military training, all the attackers were ex-military. My guess is that the members of the sleeper cells will also be ex-military. It would makes sense because they would have a base of training in weapons and tactics, both of which are necessary for what our analysts have concluded is planned," Michael answered.

As Ivan drove quickly to the Lubyanka Building, Michael used his secure mobile phone to call David Capella. He told him what he figured out and thought it might help find more suspected cell members. It was certainly important for both the CIA and the FSB to be prepared to encounter a well-trained opponent. He asked David to relay his findings to Vladimir and to tell him that he and Ivan were on their way to FSB headquarters.

David called John Henderson and John called Vladimir. The CIA and the FSB immediately linked their situation rooms, and again with full all analytic teams positioned around their respective conference tables. They shared databases and though they were separated by thousands of miles in real distance, they were electronically joined at the hip. The dual cyber force matched Chechen immigrants and visa holders in both the United States and Russia against all known Russian and Chechen military records.

The FSB suggested they narrow the match to those who would have been in the military from 1994 through 2009, which would cover the period from The First Chechen War through The Second Chechen War and the long and bloody insurgency that followed. The technique helped produce useable results quickly. They immediately found Mumadi and Rushad. There was no record of Halil having military experience, but they did match over two hundred ex-military Chechen men known to currently be in the United States and Russia.

The next step was to narrow the match to locations close to and including Landover and Moscow. The results collapsed to six possibilities in Landover and twelve in Moscow. All this took time, time that only benefited the terrorists.

Anya was one of the analysts in the FSB situation room. She had the necessary computer skills and Alexander did promise her that she would be involved. She focused on the flat panel monitor in front of her position at the large table. A headset allowed her to speak with other analysts in the room and across the link in Langley, while her fingers danced on the keyboard in the slide-out tray mounted under the table at her position. She would seamlessly alternate between fluent Russian and fluent English depending on with whom she was speaking. It was an intense effort by Anya and the entire cyber team.

Ivan and Michael arrived at the Lubyanka Building at 2:00 p.m. The chatter indicated that the attack in Moscow would take place Monday evening. Simultaneously, an attack would be initiated in Washington, D.C. that same Monday but in the morning based on the time zone difference. They had a little more than twenty-four hours left.

## Chapter 18

James Harris could not sleep. He tried all night. He looked at the alarm clock on the bed stand by his side of the king size bed in his and Denise's bedroom and saw that it was 5:00 a.m., Sunday. He turned slowly and looked at his wife of thirty-five years. He was glad to see that he had not disturbed her. How can he let her be in harm's way tomorrow? What can he do? The strategy he and Viktor developed decades ago wasn't supposed to be real. He remembered the excitement of meeting with the Russian shadowy figure, and he remembered being completely drunk. He cannot remember any of it being taken seriously at the time.

Over the years all that changed. Those plans made that night in the pub across from Lubyanka Station have now become real, or had they been real from the beginning? Viktor played the collapse of the Soviet Union like a virtuoso would play a fine violin. Viktor made a fortune producing oil and natural gas from the hundreds of thousands of energy rich acres he managed to acquire for practically nothing. It was remarkable to watch this dean of the black market from the days of the old Soviet underworld, call in every favor and debt owed to him by countless lost souls and methodically build his privately held Enerprov into a legitimate global powerhouse.

Viktor used his money and influence to help Harris rise in U.S. politics. James in turn used his increasing emerging political strength to help Viktor. Technology transferred to Enerprov, while it was denied or delayed to its competitors, provided Viktor with an endless stream of important advantages in securing undeveloped acreage. The Harris Family's energy business also benefitted from the friendship, as it was invited to participate in many of Enerprov's more lucrative deals.

Viktor never let the strategy from that night across from Lubyanka Station go unmentioned. He brought it up every time he and James were together. Often, the notebooks emerged and new entries were made. There was no doubt about it. The strategy was real; it was refined; it was perfected; and now the deadline for implementation was rapidly approaching.

The Speaker sat up in bed with his head in his hands. He turned and looked again at Denise and for the first time since meeting Viktor in 1978, he realized that he had sold his soul to the mission.

Just a short distance from the Speaker's posh home, a young dedicated Chechen Separatist was also awake in Washington's business district. Halil was used to winter in the Chechen Republic. Located on the northern slopes of the Greater Caucasus with an alpine climate and more than its share of cold and snow, the Chechen Republic endured challenging winters. An overnight drop in temperature that chilled the Washington morning air was a non-event to Halil, as he left the warmth of the deserted hotel lobby wearing only a light ski jacket and walked into the adjacent open parking garage.

He went directly to his rental car parked on the second level, but he did not open the door. Instead he knelt down and felt carefully and slowly under both the front and rear bumper. He found the attached GPS tracker under the rear bumper. The cell prepared for this possibility. He took the car key and placed it next to the tracking device, stood up and walked away from the car. He continued up three additional levels following the garage's spiral roadway. Parked, as planned, by the corner stairwell was a late model black Jeep Cherokee. He reached under the front bumper and found the key.

He unlocked the driver's door to the Jeep and sat behind the steering wheel. He took the disposable mobile phone from his jacket pocket and dialed a number. "Go?" asked the voice that answered.

"Yes," Halil said and ended the call. Halil closed the door to the Jeep, found the self-parking ticket under the driver's visor, started the engine and drove off. He paid the fee, placing cash in the machine that controlled the automated gate, and turned onto the pre-dawn Washington streets. Halil slowly made his way to Landover and to the staging site. He drove the Jeep up into the driveway of the house and pulled under the attached carport. He turned off the engine, stepped from the Jeep and covered the vehicle with a large brown tarp that was waiting in the corner of the carport. Halil stood for a moment and looked around at the abandoned development site. He then walked around to the front door of the house, unlocked it and went inside.

A few hours later, the sleeper cell member, one not connected to the mission, who was on the other end of the call, calmly walked into the parking structure of the Grand Hyatt Hotel. He went directly to Halil's rental car. He found the key, exactly where he was instructed and unlocked the car. He sat in the driver's seat, found the self-parking ticket between the visor and the headliner above him and started the engine. The driver paid the fee with cash at the automated gate and proceeded toward the Beltway.

"He is on the move," the CIA surveillance agent in Langley announced. A tail team was immediately dispatched Langley. The team, comprised of two men in a model Ford Fusion, pulled out of the Langley outdoor parking lot and headed for Washington. They were in real time contact with the GPS surveillance agent who would advise them of the subject's movement.

A few minutes later, the team was told to turn on to Interstate Route 95, where they will pick up the subject car heading south into Virginia. The car would be a little more than one mile ahead of the tail team. For almost two hours, they made sure to maintain that one mile gap as they diligently pursued the subject car.

"He is exiting in the center of Richmond, off on Exit 74C," the bored surveillance agent yawned. Several lefts and rights later, the GPS finally indicated that the subject's car had stopped and apparently parked. The tail team increased speed and hurried to the location's coordinates, only to find the car neatly parked in the self-parking area of a hotel mall complex. Expecting the subject car to stay close to D.C., the operation called for the tail team to maintain a large enough distance back so that the tail team would not be spotted. This proved a problem since the driver had enough time to walk away from the car undetected.

Halfway down Route 95 South, it became apparent that the subject may be a decoy, so the Agency alerted the team of a man and a woman, in another late model Ford Fusion, who were watching the home of Bashir Abramov. They were parked a few doors away maintaining a constant view of the Abramov home. The time reached 7:00 a.m. when they received the call that the rental car was parked in Richmond and its driver was in the wind. They had to make sure that anyone and everyone who would exit the Abramov home was closely followed. Another team, two men in a new Ford Taurus, joined them within a few minutes of the call.

The analytical team at Langley worked through the night trying to develop more intelligence on the six Chechen suspects uncovered by their analysis. All had past military experience and all are living in Landover. Two of the men have physical disabilities that would hinder their ability to participate the type of terrorist activity that was anticipated, so they were eliminated as suspects. A third man is currently in the custody of the Landover Police Department on burglary charges, not something in which a sleeper cell member would engage. A fourth man is recorded as being out of the country visiting relatives in Chechnya. Those two were also eliminated as suspects. With only two remaining people of interest, the analysts compiled files with their home addresses, places of business and vehicle information.

Two teams of FBI agents, directed by counter terrorism CIA agents, were quickly assembled and dispatched to the home addresses of the two suspected cell members. Both of the men they were seeking were indeed members of the cell, though neither the CIA nor the FBI knew that. Armed a search warrant, the first team at the home of Abbas shortly after 9:00 a.m. and found he was gone. They forced open the door of the townhouse and carefully searched inside. They found nothing.

The second team arrived at the home of Elbek, the mechanic, also around 9:00 a.m. They found only his wife and children. Two of the FBI agents approached the house with one of the CIA agents. The remaining members of the team were close by and out of sight. Having researched Elbek's professional life, when Elbek's wife answered their knock at the door, they explained to her that they were hoping Elbek could answer some questions about a car he recently serviced. The cover story was that they were part of a drug investigative unit and the car in question was identified in a recent surveillance sweep.

"I am sorry, but my husband is not here," Elbek's wife, a petite woman in her thirties with pretty dark eyes who was wearing a head scarf, explained. "He is on a religious retreat with some other Muslim men. He does this once a year. It is a ritual for these men. I do not know where he goes, but I trust my husband," she added.

"Can we reach him by phone?" one of the FBI agents asked.

"See, on the shelf in the hallway," his wife said, pointing to a small wall mounted shelf only a few feet from the front door and continued so say, "That is his phone. His car is in the garage. He completely disconnects from the modern world when he goes on these retreats. He should be home by Wednesday. You can check with his employer and they will confirm this with you. My husband is a loyal employee and always clears his schedule with his employer."

"We are sorry for bothering you and please ask your husband to call us when he returns," the same agent said. That agent then handed Elbek's wife his card with his contact information, and he and the other two agents walked away from the house. Elbek's wife closed the door. The agents got into their car and drove far out of view of Elbek's house and parked to wait for the rest of the team, who arrived in three additional cars.

"Well," exclaimed the CIA agent, a tall man with a square jaw, directing the team. "We are empty on this one, but lets' keep some eyes of that house," He added. The team brought a search warrant with them, but saw no reason to go through the house and this time. Four FBI agents, two in each of two cars, were left behind to watch the house.

What neither the Agency nor the FBI knew was that at the Landover staging site, Elbek, Abbas, Kerim and Halil all met for the first time. Kerim did not show up in the CIA's search because he had no military experience. As luck would have it for the cell, Kerim was the only other cell member to drive to the site, where he parked his car in front of the carport and covered it with a waiting brown tarp. Elbek and Abbas, without knowing their vehicles would have been followed, arrived by bus and by foot as they had always planned.

Abbas set to the task of fueling the missiles. Kerim made sure that the battery packs for the Russian

ZALA 421-12 drones, which are powered by electric motors, were charging properly. Elbek took the fueled missiles from Abbas and mounted one on each drone. Abbas coupled the canister of lethal gas to the bomb and carefully packaged it for transport. Kerim reviewed the operation of the electronic drone controls with Halil. Elbek and Abbas, both experienced in combat, would place and detonate the bomb. Kerim would remain with Halil and help pilot the drones.

Everything was ready. The men had a small cache of weapons comprised of AK-47's and MP 443 pistols and ample ammunition for all the firearms. The men will remain at the staging site until early the next day, when the mission is scheduled to begin. Bashir, at that time, will follow the instructions he finds on the website.

Unknown to Bashir, Abbas visited his home a few nights ago and picked the lock to his garage and entered. Abbas proceeded, as ordered, to and mount a small but deadly mobile phone controlled pipe bomb to the under carriage of Bashir's car. Everything was indeed ready.

In Moscow, now around 6:00 p.m., the FSB was not having much more luck than the CIA and FBI were having in the United States. Other than Service agents waiting outside of Mumadi's apartment, and surveillance on three of most likely suspects from the twelve possible suspects tagged by the broader search, they also had no suspect in hand. Despite all their excellent and rapid analytical work, each cell was one step ahead and the trails in both Moscow and Washington had gone cold.

As in Landover, the staging site in Reutov was now occupied by Rushad and three of the four cell members. The missile was fueled and mounted to the drone, the drone's battery pack was being charged, the canister of lethal gas attached to the bomb and all the electronic controls were tested and their operation reviewed. The weapon cache in Reutov was identical to that in Landover but also included several extremely powerful Russian RGO hand grenades. The main difference between the cells was that Rushad's cell members were all combat hardened ex-military and they all were as fanatical as Rushad. Both the Landover and Moscow cells were professional, well trained and dedicated. The Moscow cell was much more deadly.

Another similarity, unfortunately for Mumadi, was that his car was also rigged with a deadly mobile phone controlled pipe bomb. Mumadi kept his car parked on the street and it was easily accessible a few nights ago.

## Chapter 19

Henry and Ann Madison own a small, meticulously kept colonial home in Arlington, Virginia. Their neighborhood is a typical suburban Washington community with an equal mix of government and private-sector professionals. David Capella phoned Henry on his home phone and timed his call for when he thought Henry and Ann would be returning home following services at their Presbyterian church. They made it into the house in time to answer the phone on the fourth ring. With their only child, a twenty-year old daughter away at the University of Michigan, Sunday was a time for just Henry and his wife. He would keep the mobile phone turned off, one of the benefits of being an older staffer not concerned about career advancement. David knew this and called the house line.

"Hello?" Henry answered.

"Henry. It's Dave Capella. I'm so sorry to call you at home and to interrupt your time with Ann, but," he hesitated and then said, "It is a matter of national security. I can come out to Arlington now and meet you at the coffee shop. I promise I will not take more than twenty minutes of your day."

"A matter of national security? What am I supposed to say? Let it wait?" Henry joked. He added, "Come on out David, but please come to the house. We can speak in my study. Ann respects the few private meetings that I have at home throughout the year."

David thanked Henry, hung up the phone and left the office for his car. He covered the nine miles from Langley to Arlington in twenty minutes. Ann, thin in her fifties with chin length hair that was kept blond out of vanity, was wearing the blue dress with gray jacket she wore to church as she answered the door bell. She greeted David at the door with a welcoming smile and was truly happy to see him. Ann liked David, and knowing that he is CIA, often wondered about the secret life of Henry's 'spy' friend. "Hello David," she said. "It is good to see you. How is Carol?" she asked as they briefly hugged.

"Hello Ann, it is always a pleasure to see you. Carol is fine and misses you. We will plan a dinner soon, I promise," David said.

"Is that David?" Henry said as he walked to the door.

"Yes it is," she said. "The two of you go do your government thing in Henry's study. I already put out a tray with a pot of coffee and some cookies," she added, took David's coat and left the two men to themselves.

Henry showed David to the study, really a small living room decorated with two high back chairs on either side of a small fireplace with a slate hearth and stone surround. The chairs closed the circled configuration of two upholstered love loveseats separated by a wooden coffee table in front of the fireplace. On the table was the tray with the coffee pot, two china cups, milk and sugar service, spoons, two small plates, napkins and a large plate of recently baked chocolate chip cookies. When Ann set up coffee for her husband and a guest, she did it with precision. Dave and Henry sat on opposite loveseats facing each other,

"What is going on, Dave? Does this have something to do with your meeting yesterday with the Speaker and the conference call with Congressional leaders?" Henry asked

"Of course it does," David replied. He continued for more than the twenty minutes and told Henry about the chatter being heard by both the CIA and FSB. He told him about their analysis pointing to the real possibility of a simultaneous bombing in Moscow and Washington. David was comfortable sharing all this information with Henry. He did clear what he was going to say with John Henderson before calling Henry. The Agency knows that Henry could be trusted. He is a loyal career staffer and if anyone can keep a secret in Washington, it was Henry.

David paused long enough to pour himself some coffee, no sugar and no milk, picked up and took a healthy bite out of one of Ann's chocolate chip cookies, sipped the coffee and said, "Here's the thing Henry. We think there will also be an assassination attempt on both the President and the Vice President. We don't want to alert the Secret Service until we're sure."

Henry was stunned. "What? It all sounds clandestine," Henry said as he nervously devoured a cookie. "What does all this have to do with me?" he asked.

"It has nothing to do with you, Henry. It is about the Speaker," David answered. There was a long silence. David continued speaking slowly, "The order of succession places the Speaker in line to assume the presidency if both the President and the Vice President are unable to carry out the duties of office. That is fact number one. Speaker Harris, as you know, had a lifelong friendship with the late Viktor Chekhov. That is fact number two. The speaker and Chekhov first met in Moscow in 1978. That is fact number three. They both kept notebooks from that meeting and updated those notebooks throughout their relationship. That is fact number four. The chatter indicates that Monday, January 27th, tomorrow, is the target date. Monday would have been Chekov's seventy-fifth birthday. Those are facts number five and six. Yesterday I questioned the Speaker about this date and his reaction was unusually transparent, as if he was troubled about the date or Viktor. That is just my assumption, but his notebook, similar to the one I just referred to, was on his desk. That is fact number seven."

"Okay, where are you going with all this?" Henry asked.

"I need to see Harris' notebook," David answered.

"I am really uncomfortable with where I think you are heading, Dave," Henry said.

Without as much as taking a breath, David told, he did not ask, he told Henry, "The Agency needs you to get a look at the notebook, Henry."

Both Henry and David starred at each other in silence for more than a minute. Henry stood up and paced back and forth in front of the fireplace. He found it difficult to process what he had just heard. Okay, the Speaker was a Democrat and the President was a Republican. Okay, they opposed each other on many issues. Sure the Speaker is ambitious, but he is sixty-eight years old, extremely wealthy and with all due respect to the Vice President, the Speaker is clearly the second most powerful man in the free world, in the entire world! Why in God's name would the Speaker be part of a plot to assassinate the President and the Vice President? Henry started pacing faster and began to sweat visibly.

"Henry," David called but did not get his friend's attention. "Henry," he called again, louder and this time he stood and took Henry by the shoulders to stop him from pacing. He lowered his voice, looked Henry directly in the eyes and said, "Henry, this is real. Our country is at risk. We need to know what is written in the notebook. You have to read the notebook. We need to know what Harris and Chekhov were originally planning and we need to know how those plans matured over the years."

Henry took a deep breath, looked at his friend and calmly responded, "I don't know if I can do it. It is an evasion of privacy. It is a violation of trust. Dave, I worked for the Speaker for the past fifteen years. He and I have a professional relationship, but we are also friends. I know him as a tough politician, but also as a good man. I respect the CIA and I respect you. I'd like to think that I can actually help stop any credible threat of terror, but please, I am a simple career Washington staffer. You are asking me to do something that is so far from who I am, and you are asking me to do this to a friend. I can't do it. I can't." Henry turned from David and started to pace again.

"Henry, please stop and look at me," David said, once again reaching out and holding Henry's shoulders to stop him from pacing. He continued, "Henry. Listen to me, please. Your country needs you to do this. I am sorry but you are the only person who can access the notebook in time for its information to help avert the death of innocent Americans, and possibly even stop an assassination attempt on our leadership. You are the only person Henry. I am sorry, but you have to trust me that this is the right thing to do. Have you ever seen the notebook?" David said. He thought he would approach the subject differently to help Henry calm down.

"I have seen the notebook. I first saw it when Jim met with Chekhov about ten years ago and then at another meeting just before Viktor died. I did not see it again until about one month ago. The Speaker has been bringing it to the office on a daily basis since then. I agree with you that there is definitely something about that notebook that is bothering him. Are you sure there is a connection?" He asked.

"The Agency is sure and I am sure," David answered.

"Alright, I will try to read the notebook, but when and how? If you are right and everything is planned for tomorrow when will I have time to look at the notebook?" Henry asked.

"The Speaker has a meeting tonight with the Minority Leader of the Senate, correct" David asked.

"Yes. They are both Democrats and this is a regularly scheduled session. They meet once each quarter. They alternate the meetings at each other's office, have a drink and talk for about an hour. The meeting tonight is at 6:00 p.m. and in the Speaker's office. Afterward they will leave and have dinner at a nearby restaurant," Henry answered.

"You are scheduled to be there for the meeting?

"Yes. I make sure that everything goes as planned and on time, but I wait outside during the meeting. When they leave for dinner, I go home. They always go home after dinner as well, so I lock up the suite before I leave."

"The Speaker arrives about a half an hour before the meeting?"

"Yes"

"We need to hope that he brings the notebook with him. My guess is that he will. When I met with him yesterday, I noticed that the notebook was on his desk. Harris is predictable and will most likely walk into the office and, if he has the notebook with him, place it on the desk. When the Speaker comes out of his office to greet the Minority Leader, you will have enough time to move the notebook. Put it someplace else in the office. Most likely with the notebook out of sight, Harris will forget it long enough to leave without it when he and the Minority Leader go for dinner. When they walk out, you pick up the notebook, read it and then replace it where Harris left it. You then simply leave his office. Be prepared that the Speaker might remember the notebook as he is about to leave the building. He will come back for it. Therefore you need to spend no more than a few minutes reading it, replacing it, and getting out of his office," David carefully laid out the plan for Henry.

"I think you're right. When the Speaker and the Minority Leader start talking, especially when they are leaving together, they usually get lost in their wrangle. They are always joking and laughing. But I agree that as the conversation quiets on the way out of the building the Speaker will go through a mental checklist relative to his routine. I have been with him long enough to know how he thinks. He will remember the notebook. I will not have more than five minutes, if I have that much time at all."

"That will have to be enough time," David said and asked, "Can I count on you Henry? Will you do this for your country?"

"I will try. I am terribly conflicted, but I will try," Henry answered. "How can we be sure that the Speaker will bring the notebook this evening?" he asked.

"That is in God's hands Henry," David answered. "Assuming you have the chance to read the notebook, call me as soon as you leave the office and I will instruct you from that point on," he added. He explained to Henry that he would be in his office in Langley, waiting for the call.

"I will have a team here, parked outside of your home and hidden from Ann's view. She will have no idea that the agents are here. She will be well protected and completely safe. I will also have a team waiting to follow you back to Langley," David said.

"I like the team here with Ann but please promise me that there will be no CIA near the Rayburn

Building? I don't want even the slightest unusual activity. Promise me, please Dave?" Henry pleaded.

David reluctantly agreed on a forgoing CIA presence at the Rayburn Building but reaffirmed that agents will be stationed outside Henry's Arlington home. He assured Henry that everything will work out. David thanked Henry and the two men walked to the door. Ann, seeing Henry and David leaving the study, retrieved David's coat and handed it to him at the door. David smiled at Ann as he took his coat, shook Henry's hand and left their Arlington home.

## Chapter 20

Michael waited for others in the FSB situation room to leave before he stood up. Anya was taking a break from her terminal at the table and she walked directly to Michael. She resisted the temptation to hug him, but smiled and touched his left forearm with her right hand. He returned the subtle greeting and they left the room together. They walked to her cubicle where Michael expressed his concern for Anya's safety, but was happy to see her involved with her colleagues working on the situation. "I understand how important it is to be involved and how difficult it is to wait," he said. "Are you feeling as good as you appear to be?" he added.

"Yes. I am really fine. I have to admit that I don't know whether to feel fear because they wanted to kill me, or to be angry about it. I admit that I am afraid, angry and still filled with grief over the murder of my father and my uncle," Anya replied. "I am good, but confused," she added and continued with, "The kindness in your note last night made me feel less frightened, less angry and less alone. I thank you so much for that note."

"Do you have more family, Anya?" Michael asked.

"I do. Actually, I have a big family, many cousins, aunts and uncles and we all keep in touch," she said with a smile, and added, "They are all good people;

engineers, teachers, even a doctor, but I am the only FSB."

"That's good. There is no substitute for family," Michael said.

Anya hesitated, looked Michael in the eye, and said to him, "Earlier today I read our complete file on you, beyond the information I was first provided, sorry, but I was curious and I wanted to know more about this mysterious American who saved my life. I am so, so, sorry about your wife and your little girl. God must cry giant tears for the actions of some people."

"It was a long time ago, but it still hurts as though it was yesterday. Yes, God must cry giant tears," Michael answered. He added, "I miss them both, but I especially miss all of what could have been for my daughter. I try hard not to, but I cannot help thinking about how she would have grown up and all that she would have accomplished. I wonder what would have made her cry and what would have made her laugh. I wonder about how she would have handled all the normal phases and challenges of life."

Anya responded with, "I understand."

At that moment Michael and Anya felt a bond that would last a lifetime. It was the kind of bond that is normal between family members. Michael was not a replacement for Oleg and neither was Anya a replacement for Cindy. They forged a bond that was much more than a friendship but far less than a love affair. They formed that special relationship that few people unrelated by blood and not romantically involved have the blessing to achieve. They knew at that moment that they could rely on the each other for the rest of their lives.

It was getting late and everyone in The Lubyanka Building was bracing for the next day. The FSB needed to have its best people fresh and ready to think and to act. Innocent lives were at risk. The leadership of two major world powers might be facing assassination attempts. Anya's security came by and waited till she securely logged off of the system, picked up her purse, briefcase and coat. She said goodnight to Michael and left with her two FSB protectors. She would return early Monday morning and perform her duty as part of the analytical team.

Ivan walked over to Michael and noting that the time was approaching 7:00 p.m., asked if he was hungry. Michael, watching Anya and her security team leave the area, turned to Ivan and said, "Yes. I bet you have a suggestion?"

"I do," said Ivan, with a sly smile.

For the next few hours, Michael and Ivan enjoyed some basic, but extremely delicious, Russian food at a small nearby eatery. Both men purposely nursed a single Baltika each, keeping their respective alcohol intake to just that one beer. They were unsure of what was coming the next day but they knew that it would come fast and it would be aggressive. They wanted to be ready.

Michael, still hoping there was some way to get an edge on the terror that was being forecast in the chatter, asked Ivan about the possibility of the FSB pushing Andrei Chekhov a little and perhaps forcing his hand. "There has to be a path to Andrei. If we could get even some small reaction from him, it could lead to much more," he said.

Ivan explained to Michael that his level within the Service was not privileged to that information, but knew enough to say, "The Service, much like your CIA, is a cross between independent patriots and political hacks. Politicians control the budget, so they often win. Regarding Andrei Chekhov and Enerprov, many in the political arena owe him and his company their careers. They protect him and they protect Enerprov," he said, but added, "However if anyone senses a weakness or a possible opening, they will be quick to abandon Andrei. In fact, they would enjoy abandoning him. The problem is that there appears to be little chance of that. Hence, my American friend, even this low level loyal patriot of the Service can tell you that there is no way we can pressure Andrei."

Michael listened intently to Ivan, but could not accept how Andrei was so completely protected. He thought about Pavel and how he sensed something honorable about this man, something that was not for sale. Michael thought that Pavel was their path to Andrei, he was sure of it. The opening to Pavel would be Rushad, since Pavel made it clear that he had no respect for Rushad. Michael knew that he could not exclude Ivan, so he decided to tell him what he was thinking. He started with, "Pavel, Enerprov's Head of Security, does not like Rushad and I got the impression that Pavel is not comfortable with the closeness between Rushad and Andrei."

"Where are you going with this Mr. Clark?" Ivan asked.

"I want to speak with Pavel and see if he would be willing to help."

"Nyet! We cannot do that!"

"Please calm down Ivan. I sense that Pavel is a patriot. We need to do something; otherwise the terrorists will control the pace of everything that happens and people will die," Michael pleaded.

Ivan thought about what Michael said. He picked up his mobile phone and called Vladimir. The conversation was in Russian and it was long. Ivan handed the phone to Michael, after what seemed like an hour but was only a few minutes.

Vladimir said to Michael, "I know Pavel. We served together in Afghanistan in 1980. He is a patriot, but he is also loyal to his employer. I respect your instincts Mike and I share your concern. I will allow this, but I will call Pavel. I will make it official and share with him that there is chatter. I will also share that there may be a link to Andrei's father and that Andrei may know something that can save lives. I have to leave it at that and trust Pavel to connect the dots. I will have to share with him that you are more than a consultant. Are you willing to take that risk? Is Henderson willing to take that risk? It may even get back to your day job, and I bet Bricksen Grove has no idea of your, how do you Americans call it, moonlighting?"

"I am willing to take the risk, but I cannot speak for the Agency or anyone connected with it. I am not concerned about Bricksen Grove and if I am right about Pavel, Bricksen Grove will not find out. Back to the Agency, I am an independent and," he hesitated and continued, "I don't always follow the rules."

"I do follow the rules," Vladimir said. "I have to call Henderson first. Give me ten minutes."

The call ended and the next ten minutes were uncomfortable. Ivan was not happy and he showed his feelings. Michael understood Ivan's perspective, but he was sure that his instincts about Pavel were right and he understood that Pavel may be their only chance to take control of the situation from the terrorists. Finally, Michael's encrypted mobile phone rang.

"This is Mike," he said, answering it on the first ring.

"You better be sure about this Mike," said David Capella on the other end of the call. "Henderson ripped me a new one. However, he agreed that we have to try. I have some action working here as well. Vladimir is speaking to Pavel now. Wait where you are until you receive a call from Pavel. You are on your own from there. Vlad will call Ivan as well, so he knows to stick with you like glue." David said and concluded with, "Good luck Mike." With that, the call ended.

Ivan's phone rang and a short conversation in Russian followed. Ivan smiled as he ended the call and leaned over the table to Michael and said, "I am with you Mr. Clark." Michael laughed and thanked Ivan as his own phone rang again. This time it was Pavel and they agreed to meet at Enerprov in thirty minutes, at about 10:00 p.m. Michael and Ivan left the little restaurant and went straight to Enerprov.

Pavel, holding his coat over one arm, was waiting for them in the lobby. He was speaking to the two night shift guards behind the security desk and they seemed to be having a light hearted conversation. Pavel related well to all people, and his personal outreach was something Michael noticed during his protocol review relative to his Bricksen Grove engagement.

Ivan and Michael walked through the revolving door and Pavel quickly turned toward them offering his hand. "Hello again Mr. Clark," Pavel said. He added, "I knew there was more to you than we were told. Vladimir says our country is at risk and that I can trust you. You should be honored. A stranger having Vladimir's trust is a big deal. Come with me. We will go to my office." He looked at Ivan and said, "Please, wait here. I do not want FSB images on the internal security footage recorded on the other side of this security desk."

Ivan understood and walked back to the revolving door and stood to the side with his arms folded. He watched as Pavel and Michael stepped into the elevator and then alternated his attention between the lobby and the street.

Michael and Pavel walked into Pavel's office threw their coats on his couch and sat down. Pavel sat behind his desk and Michael sat across from him. "A CIA independent, frankly I would have guessed regular CIA," Pavel began. Michael gave a guarded smile and listened as Pavel continued, "Vlad says our countries have a real threat. Our leaders have a real threat. He says that Rushad is most likely involved, which does not surprise me one bit. But Andrei? I am not so sure. Vlad told me about the meeting with Viktor Chekhov and your Speaker Harris. I don't understand why Viktor, his son or Speaker Harris would be involved in the madness that Vlad says is indicated by the chatter. He said you will explain. I am listening Mike."

"Thank you for meeting with me, Pavel. I am sure Vladimir explained that Bricksen Grove has no idea of how I spend my time outside of their employ. They know nothing about my work with the CIA and it needs to remain that way," Michael said. He continued, "I understand your skepticism. We know that Chekhov Sr. and Harris were close and were helpful to each other. Viktor's wealth and influence helped Harris to rise politically. Harris, in turn, used his political position to help make sure that American technology was available to Enerprov. Harris' family also benefitted financially. All of that is known and is a matter of record. It is the way the world works. However, we believe," Michael paused, "I believe, that Viktor and Harris had dreamed up some sort of strategy that would force a dual power shift. I think it has to be that big because, and I agree with you, why else would they take a treasonous step like the one we are hearing about in the chatter?"

"Okay. So we agree about the enormity of the plot. Why am I here?"

"A notebook; Andrei has a notebook that his father kept current right up to his death. We believe, and

I am now saying 'we,' that the notebook has the answer. Have you seen Andrei with an old leather bound notebook?" Michael asked.

Pavel leaned back in his chair, pushing back from the desk. His facial expression changed from skepticism to concern. He put one hand around his chin and said, "Yes. I saw the notebook for the first time when Viktor Chekhov died. Andrei would bring it with him to the office almost every time when he was in Moscow. I never asked him about it. I had not seen it again for over three years until last month. Andrei started bringing it with him daily. I am afraid that is all I can tell you about the notebook Mike," he concluded.

"Pavel, we need to see the notebook."

"Impossible. Andrei most likely has it in his apartment here in the city, but can also have it at his estate in the country or at one of his other homes around the globe. Regardless, even if we agree that it is in his apartment, how would we get it?"

"I was hoping you would have the answer to that question," Michael challenged Pavel.

After an uncomfortable silence and Pavel's unbreakable stare, Pavel leaned forward and said, "I do have the answer. My guess is that if Andrei is involved, and I caution you that I say if. If he is involved, then he will have the notebook with him tomorrow. Viktor had an interesting characteristic. He wrote down everything he was planning and everything he accomplished. If you are correct that the notebook contents include a plan that aligns with the chatter, than Andrei will have to have the notebook with him tomorrow so that he could make the final acknowledgement for his father. I believe he will have the notebook with him because he is planning on leaving the office early, around 4:00 p.m., to go to his country home. I made the security arrangements, which is why I know his plans. My staff escorted Andrei's wife and children out of the city Friday afternoon. Hence, he will need to have the notebook with him while traveling to the country so that he could make the entry."

Pavel took a breath and continued, "I suppose I could find a reason to delay Andrei and keep him in the city. As we get closer to the event, Andrei will become agitated and perhaps that will open an opportunity to get him to produce the notebook. He may feel his father's compulsion to note a change in the plan? That is what Viktor would have done. I will have eyes on him and as soon as that notebook is seen, we will find a way to get our hands on it. I may even find an excuse for me to speak with him directly, but I am afraid that is the best I could do."

"It will have to be, Pavel," Michael said. "Any advance time we get, even minutes, will be more that we have now. I understand how difficult this is for you Pavel," Michael added, paused and continued, "You are a patriot and it is an honor to know you, Sir."

Both men stood up, picked up their coats and left the office.

Outside, as Michael and Ivan left Enerprov, a man smoking a cigarette a short way from the Enerprov Building reached for his mobile phone and punched in a number. "It is the American," he said to the person answering the call and added, "He has FSB with him."

Rushad, alone in an empty room of the house at the Reutov staging site, was the person on the other end of the call. He dared not leave the staging site, but that didn't mean he couldn't call on minor cell members, not connected with the mission, to provide him with information. Rushad replied, "Good job, go home. I will take it from here." He ended that call walked into an adjacent room where the other cell members were sitting. He announced, "A small change in plans. I will accompany the bomb team tomorrow. We need to get Oleg's daughter for insurance. I need to be out there to find her. I arranged a safe house close to our primary bomb site for just this contingency. We only need one person to handle the drone." The cell members accepted the change to the operation and pledged to follow Rushad's lead. Rushad, stood there and thought to himself. "I have unfinished business with this American and there will be time to take care of that after we achieve honor tomorrow."

## Chapter 21

Speaker Harris arrived at his office suite promptly at 5:30 p.m., exactly thirty minutes before his meeting with Minority Leader Evert Jackson. Henry, as usual, had the suite open and was waiting. "Good Evening Henry, my friend. Thank you for interrupting your Sunday evening to help with Evert," James said, as he walked by Henry and into his private office. Henry followed the Speaker into the office.

"Mr. Speaker, Senator Jackson will be here on time and here are the issues I see as priorities that you should discuss with him," Henry said, He handed the Speaker a sheet of paper with three meeting topics and associated comments printed on it.

"Come on Henry; hold the Mr. Speaker crap for when Evert shows up. While it is just us Oklahoma boys, please let's keep it 'Jim' and 'Henry,' okay?"

"Sorry, Jim, force of habit," Henry laughed.

"Good. Let me see your comments," James said. He took the paper with one hand, after throwing his coat on his couch. In his other hand, The Speaker was holding his small briefcase. Henry said he would get some additional material and left the office. Jim used that opportunity to remove a few items from his briefcase, including the notebook. He held the notebook in his hand and stared at it for a moment, took a deep breath, and then he carefully placed the notebook in the same corner of his desk as he has been doing recently. Henry, watching from outside the Speaker's office, saw it all. Henry waited a second and then walked back into the office.

"Jim," Henry said, "My opinion is that you need to press the Minority Leader on the first issue. We need to know if we have the votes. The other issues are for you to use in the conversation." The Speaker smiled and said he agreed. The two men discussed strategy for the meeting, reviewed where James and Evert would meet for dinner and found a moment for some friendly banter before they heard the loud voice of Senator Jackson. James told Henry that he would go and welcome his guest himself.

Henry had a few seconds. He was holding folders of information relative to the issues he compiled for the meeting. He placed the folders over the notebook, completely hiding it from view.

"Good Evening Sir," Henry said as the Speaker and the Minority Leader walked into the office.

"Hey Henry," Senator Jackson, a tall, heavy set man from North Carolina, said with a touch of the South in his voice. "I understand that you run the House, and Jim is merely your prop," he added.

"That is absolutely correct. But the Speaker gets to go to all the parties," Henry joked.

The Speaker spoke up in a serious tone, "All kidding aside, without Henry the House would be a mess. He is a good man and a good friend." The Speaker and Senator Jackson walked into James' office and sat down in the chairs opposite the Speaker's desk. Henry said he would remain outside through their meeting if they needed any information to assist their discussion. He turned and left the office, closing the door behind him.

The next hour seemed like a lifetime. Henry's conflicts were made more difficult to deal with by the Speaker's kind comments about Henry's professional value and his remarks about their friendship. He knew that David Capella would not have asked for his help if it was not truly necessary. But the thought of his friend James Harris being involved in the kind of treason that David suggested, was really hard for Henry to handle. Henry spent the entire hour in the outer office staring at the Speaker's door across the reception floor. He fought back his anxiety over what he had agreed to do for David, and he did his best to remain focused on following through on his promise to help.

The door of the Speaker's office opened and the laughter of the Speaker and the Minority Leader grew louder as they walked from the office with their coats on. "We have the votes in the Senate, Henry," the Speaker shouted to Henry. "Tomorrow morning, make the call and let the Whip know he has to get our people in the House lined up. Tell him I will come to the chamber to meet with him in the morning," he instructed and added, "Good Night Henry. Please thank Ann for sharing you with the American People tonight." The Speaker and the Minority Leader left the suite.

The clock started. Henry would have no more than five minutes, if that much time. He had rehearsed his actions for the past hour. He would only use one or two minutes. He would quickly scan the notebook and get out. Unfortunately, Henry found himself unable to move. But the clock had no such problem. Time was going by and he had to act and act now. He was so nervous that his forehead filled with beads of sweat. Henry took several breaths, walked into the Speaker's office and reached for the notebook under the folders. He opened it and calmed down as he read the early notes.

"November 15, 1978, Lubyanka Station, Moscow Russia: Viktor Chekhov of the USSR, James Harris of the USA; meeting as citizens of our respective countries," the opening notes read. USSR referring to the former Union of Soviet Socialists Republics, all separate sovereign nations today. Henry continued to scan through the description of the pub and other factual notes until he came to, "Our strategy, which we both declare as necessary for our world, is to take the steps necessary to collapse the leadership of each super power and have one combined superior power emerge." The notes that followed detailed those steps. There was much written about how to obtain wealth and political power, and how Viktor and James would assist each other to achieve both. Other steps were more sinister and described how a simultaneous assassination of the leader of the USSR and the USA would open a pathway to seize control and merge the super powers. The notes pointed to this coming January 29th, Viktor's seventy-fifth birthday, as the longest they would wait to implement the strategy.

Henry, noticing the time, started scanning more than reading and quickly turned through the pages. He slowed as he found the entries made just prior to Viktor's death. They read, "February 20, 2011; Washington D.C.: Viktor has a network of Chechen Separatists, whom he distains but knows he could exploit; He has the wealth and I am positioned politically; It will take more time to have things in place; January 27th would now be a real operational date."

There was an entry made about Viktor's death and there was a note about Andrei, "Viktor's son,

Andrei, is a mad man. He actually wants to do this. I thought it was all over when Viktor died, but Andrei is crazy. He believes that he needs to implement the strategy to honor his father. He also hates the Chechens, but recognizes their usefulness and their willingness to follow the strategy to the end. Andrei said he would make everything public if I don't do my part. I have no choice."

Henry turned to the most recent entries and found them to be chilling, "Bombs will be placed in busy Metro stations in both Moscow and D.C. They will be placed to detonate simultaneously, during the evening rush in Moscow aligned to the morning rush in D.C. The bombs will release a chemical agent, but the death toll will be limited. The purpose of the bombs is to create a diversion, confusion and fear. The real targets are the President of the United States and the President of the Federation of Russia. Drones will be used for the assassinations. The Vice President of the United States will also be targeted, resulting in me, as Speaker of the House, succeeding to the presidency. Andrei's man, Viktor's choice, will become the Russian president and all the elements of the union will be in place. The selected Metro stations will be close to the targets in both countries but the operatives will have flexibility to choose other stations depending on circumstances on that day. The leaders will be hit while they are being moved. The confusion following the bombings will be our advantage and the drones will not be detected until it is too late to stop them."

Henry read the final entry, penned this past Friday "I learned today that Denise is going to be in D.C. on the day, January 27<sup>th</sup>. I have no way to assure her protection. I am so sorry that I have been part of this all these years and I cannot believe that I am still part of it. I have no choice. Andrei will reveal everything and my entire family will be destroyed with the shame of my treason. My only option is to succeed. I am so sorry Denise, please forgive me, I love you."

Henry was in shock. He was reading James' words, written in his own hand. He was reading a confession to treason. Oddly enough, Henry was calm. He felt more anger than fear and now his goal was getting this information to David and the CIA. He closed the notebook and put it back on the desk where the Speaker had first placed it. He picked up the folders and began to walk out of the office and suddenly found himself looking directly into James Harris's eyes.

"Henry. I'm glad you're still here. I do not have my keys with me and I forgot something," the Speaker said giving no indication as to whether or not he saw Henry with the notebook. "You needed something from my office Henry?" he asked.

"Just my notes, Jim," Henry answered lifting the folders to make his point.

"Well, give me one minute and then you can lock up," James said as he walked into his office, picked up the notebook and placed it in his briefcase. "All set," James said. He smiled at Henry and left the suite.

Henry slowly walked to his desk and put the folders down. He was not sure about what the Speaker may have seen. He couldn't worry about that now. He had to call David and tell him about what he read. He thought it best to leave and call David from the car.

James Harris left the Rayburn Building and walked over to the waiting car and driver. The Minority Leader was in the back seat waiting for his host so that they could continue to the restaurant and dinner. The Speaker opened the car door and told Senator Jackson that he needed to make a quick call and then they would be on their way. He walked a few feet behind the car and used his mobile phone to call the emergency number.

"Yes," the voice on the other end of the call said.

"My chief of staff, Henry Madison, needs to be dealt with."

"I have it," the voice said and Jim ended the call. He walked back to the car and joined the Minority Leader in the back seat and the driver proceeded to take them to the restaurant.

The voice at the other end of the call belonged to Halil, who immediately made another call to the same cell operative who drove the rental car to Richmond. He described Henry Madison and Henry's 2013 government issued white Ford Taurus. The operative, waiting in a dark late model Toyota sedan, was only a few minutes away from the Rayburn Building. He was assigned to stay close to the Speaker in case of an emergency. The operative drove to where he was told Henry would be parked and made it in time to see Henry driving out of the garage. He turned his car around and pulled behind Henry and began to follow him.

On the passenger seat across from the operative was a stacked array of electronics. One device was a digital scanner, another was a transmitter and the third a laptop computer. The driver engaged the electronics and brought everything live as he followed Henry through the streets of Washington and on to the Beltway.

Henry called David's private number at Langley, with David picking up on the first ring. "Dave," Henry said, excited by a tremendous release of adrenalin. He added nervously, "You were right Dave. You were right."

"Henry, come directly to Langley. Keep talking to me and tell me everything you know. I will put my phone on record," David said as he hit the record button to start the integral record feature on his phone.

"The Speaker saw me coming out of his office. You were right that he would forget the notebook briefly and then come back for it. I don't know if he saw me with the notebook and I want to be sure Ann is protected. Are your people with Ann?"

"Our people have been in front of your house for the past hour Henry. We have three agents there. Ann is safe," David said as John Henderson walked into this office, after he received an e-mail from David that he was on the phone with Henry. Like David, John was at Langley waiting for Henry's call.

"Thank you. I read most of the notes. There really wasn't much written in the notebook considering all the years that have passed. But what is there is clear," Henry told David and continued to relay all he could remember about the diversion bombs, the chemical agent, the assassination targets and the drones. He confirmed from the notes that the operatives are Chechen Separatists and that the objective of the strategy was a union between the Russian Federation and the United States.

All of a sudden, Henry's car started to accelerate on its own. "Dave, my car is acting strange. It is going faster even though I have my foot off the accelerator and on the break. I am having a difficult time controlling it," Henry said as he had to steer his accelerating car around the few cars in front of him on the Beltway. Henry did not notice the car following him, also accelerating and steering around cars in order to stay close behind him.

John Henderson immediately shouted to agents outside of David's office, "Have the FBI get a chopper and a sniper in the air over the Beltway. They are looking for a 2013 government issued white Ford Taurus. Behind it they will see a pursuit vehicle. Tell them they have to eliminate the pursuit vehicle. Tell the FBI to order the local police to shut down all Beltway entrances from Capitol Hill to Langley. Tell them to have the police clear the Beltway of all traffic in front of that Taurus."

John and David knew exactly what was going on. The computer control units on Henry's car were hacked into using the car's emergency GPS locator and distress link. The hacker, the operative behind him, only needed to stay close enough to maintain the connection between his transmitter and Henry's GPS. He had full control of the Henry's electronic controlled fuel injection system and was signally it to draw more fuel and thereby accelerate. The operative's next move was to render the antilock-breaks unworkable by confusing their electronic controls and forcing them to fail. It was only a matter of time and Henry would be completely powerless to do anything to retain control of his car.

"Henry, do you see a car following you in your rear view mirror?" David asked.

"I do. What is happening?"

"Stay calm Henry. We have a chopper in the air and it will be there in seconds. Keep steering and stay on the road."

"I am trying, but I am still accelerating. Damn it, I going 100 miles per hour; 105; 110. What should I do? My breaks were helping but now they are fighting me as well. I can't turn the engine off and the electronic parking break is indicating a malfunction. Please help me Dave. I'm scared Dave. I never drove this fast. Please Dave. Help me!"

Just then an FBI helicopter started to descend on both cars. The chopper had a light beacon mounted under its frame and shined its bright light on the pursuit vehicle. The FBI ordered the local police to quickly close all Beltway entrances ahead of Henry and also to rid the roadway of other cars. Soon, there was only an empty road in front of Henry. The pursuit vehicle ignored the chopper as its driver continued to stay close to Henry. The operative was able to confuse Henry's antilock breaking system into malfunction, as he commanded more power from the fuel injection system. Henry's car accelerated to 120 miles per hour and Henry did all he could to keep it on the road.

It was too dangerous to attempt to get between the vehicles at this rate of speed. The only chance was for the FBI chopper to stop the pursuit vehicle in hope of Henry's car getting far enough ahead to break the signal. The pilot lowered the chopper enough to give the sniper, sitting behind him, a clear view of the operative. The sniper lifted his rifle, a fully automatic M4, to his shoulder and took careful aim through the high powered optic mounted on the weapon. The M4 is not the best sniper weapon for a stealthy operation, but this shot is not about stealth; it is all about a quick kill. The fire power of the M4 is perfectly suited for this objective.

"Dave. Please help me. I can't control the car any more, I can't," Henry pleaded. Suddenly, as his car continued to race forward, Henry felt a strange calm. "Dave. Please tell Ann I love her. Tell her I had to do this for my country," Henry said, choking back tears as his car accelerated over 130 miles per hour and was weaving all over the road. The operative's car was following closely.

The command to the sniper in his ear piece was crystal clear and urgent, "Eliminate the target now." The pilot leveled the chopper and held it perfectly steady only a few feet to the side and a few feet above the operative's car. The sniper fired several rounds, each of them hitting the operative who fell dead as his car spun out of control, flipping several times and then exploding into flames.

The chopper lifted higher to follow Henry. There was nothing that anyone could do now but pray. Henry's car was at maximum speed and barreling forward toward an overpass. The signal was broken but before Henry could regain functional control, his car slammed into the abutment of the overpass at a speed in excess of 130 miles per hour. The fireball said it all. The phone in David's office fell silent as an unlikely American hero, to quote President Ronald Reagan's use of the words of American aviator John Gillespie Magee, Jr. following the 1986 Space Shuttle Challenger disaster, "slipped the surly bonds of earth to touch the face of God."

David looked at John and both men did not say a word. A crowd of agents and others gathered by David's office door stood perfectly still and perfectly quiet. The pilot, a tear rolling down his cheek, kept the chopper hovering about the burning wreck of Henry's car. The sniper, with his M4 in his lap, saluted the fallen comrade he had never met.

Chapter 22

John Henderson was the first to regain composure. "Let's get the link live and get me I Vladimir on the phone," he screamed, as he hurried from David's office pushing his way through the crowd of CIA staffers. He went directly to the situation room. David quickly called one of the agents outside of Ann and Henry's home on the agent's mobile phone and ordered her and the other agents to go inside to Ann. He instructed the agent that once inside, she should hand the phone to Ann. David could not leave Langley and he had to tell Ann himself, she deserved to hear it from him even if he had to tell her over the phone.

Ann was startled when she answered the door to find the two women and one man showing her their credentials. One of the women agents gently asked if she and Ann could go and sit down. Ann directed them into the dining room. Ann sat down at the table and the agent pulled a chair around and sat right next to her. The agent then handed her mobile phone to Ann.

"Ann. This is Dave. I am so sorry Ann. I am so sorry," Dave said. He did his best to tell Ann as gently as possible. But there was no approach soft enough to tell this woman that her husband of so many years was not coming home, that this man who spent his professional life behind a desk in Washington had just died for his country. Ann started to cry uncontrollably dropping the phone to the floor. The female agent sitting beside her hugged her closely. The other female agent picked up the phone and left the room. David ordered the agents to stay with Ann. The Agency also dispatched a psychological trauma team to assist.

The Speaker and Senator Jackson were seated at their regular table in a small Italian restaurant only a few minutes from the Capitol. The owner made his usual fuss over his distinguished guests as the men sat down and ordered drinks, bourbon straight up for Jackson and scotch and water for the Speaker. They toasted their efforts for the legislation under immediate consideration and then James said, "Would you excuse me for a few seconds? See if there is anything on this menu that we should avoid tonight. That is what we will order when I get back."

The Speaker reached into his briefcase, which he brought with him, and took the notebook in his hand. He walked over to the owner of the restaurant and whispered to him, "I need a burn barrel."

The owner smiled, he knew when not to ask his powerful customers questions, and walked him through the kitchen and out a side door to the alley. A member of the kitchen staff followed, on instructions from the owner, carrying a small metal pail and a can of flammable oil. They left the Speaker alone and went back into the restaurant.

James put the pail on the ground. He tore all the pages from the notebook and placed them in the pail along with the leather cover and spine of the notebook. He poured all the oil on the torn notebook and used a match from a box of matches he took from the owner to ignite the contents of the pail.

There on the ground in the alley, James watched the last thirty-six years of his life go up in a controlled flame. He knew that Andrei still had Viktor's notebook and that his own signatures were in that notebook as well, but he was sure that Andrei would not make the mistake he did and leave the notebook for someone to find and to read. This was good. With his notebook destroyed and Andrei's secure, there was no hard evidence. James had no idea what happened to Henry, but he knew Henry had seen the notebook and had to be stopped and that the Chechen thugs would do their worst. James knew there was blood on his hands but his only thoughts were for his own survival. He felt safer seeing the notebook destroyed.

James went back to the table and shared drinks and laughs with Senator Jackson. They ordered dinner and everything appeared normal until they were interrupted by a young man, another member of the Speaker's staff, who came rushing into the restaurant. He approached the table and said, "Mr. Speaker. There has been a terrible accident on the Beltway and Mr. Madison is dead. I am sorry Sir."

This was the news that James knew would come, but prayed would not. He told Jackson that he had to leave and offered to have his driver take the Minority Leader home. Jackson refused, said he would have the owner call him a taxi and he would be fine. He told James to go and do what was necessary.

James thanked the young man and asked him if he heard how Ann was doing. The staffer told him that she was being attended to and that for some reason the CIA was involved. He said the police phoned the on-call number to report about Henry and told him that the CIA was with Henry's wife. He said to the Speaker, "The police told me that Ann has several people around her, including members of the CIA. The police were called about an out-of-control car on the Beltway and were asked to clear the path in front of the car. The officer said the call came from the CIA and that when they sent officers to the Madison home, CIA agents told them everything with Ann was under control."

"I assume the CIA is involved because Henry was my chief-of-staff. It is most likely a simple precaution and nothing more. You stay here and make sure Senator Jackson gets his taxi," the Speaker said. James then walked out of the restaurant to his car. The driver was standing there holding a rear door open. The Speaker sat down in the back and the driver closed the door, went around to the front and got in the driver's seat, put the car in gear and drove off.

Speaker Harris waited until he was home and face-to-face with Denise to tell her about the terrible accident that took Henry. She suggested that they immediately go to Ann. The Speaker agreed with his wife and they went directly to Arlington. The CIA agent at the front door let the Harris' inside. Denise went directly to Ann, now sitting in the study, sat next to her and hugged the grief stricken woman. The Speaker stood and expressed his sorrow in words.

After about thirty minutes, the medical personnel with Ann suggested that they let her rest. The Speaker and Denise agreed and left the home. On the way back in the car, Denise asked the question that James knew was coming, "CIA agents? What is going on Jim?"

"I will find out tomorrow my love," James said. "Maybe you should cancel the fund raiser?" he asked.

"Let's see in the morning. I can only think of Ann right now," she answered. The ride back to their home continued in silence.

Once back at the residence, the Speaker found it difficult to sleep. He first thought about Henry but quickly turned his thinking to all that was planned for the next day. The more his mind raced the less he thought about Henry, Ann and even Denise. All he could think of was taking the oath and stepping into the presidency. His soul was completely gone.

## Chapter 23

It was almost 4:30 a.m. Monday morning in Moscow, when Vladimir awoke in bed to answer his mobile phone. He listened to everything John told him about the notebook, thanked him and said he would be at the Lubyanka Building within an hour. Immediately following the call with John, Vladimir called Alexander. He ordered the link in full operation and told Alexander he wanted the best agents and analysts at their posts by 6:00 a.m. He quickly showered to make sure he was fully awake, dressed and went to the car waiting for him.

Around the same time that Vladimir was awakened by John Henderson, Michael's mobile phone rang. It was David Capella calling to say, "You were right Mike, the Speaker is in this up to his eyeballs, the damn son-of-a-bitch!"

Michael, hearing the anger in David's voice, asked, "Dave, what's wrong?"

"You remember me talking about my friend Henry Madison; a gentle man; a good man who never hurt a soul? Harris's chief-of-staff? I asked him to try to read the notebook. It was something that was completely out of his comfort zone. On top of that, he worked for the Speaker for the past fifteen years. I pressured him Mike. I appealed to his patriotism. He finally agreed. He did a great job. He read the notebook. He called me and told me about what he read. All our analysis about the chatter was confirmed. A simultaneous attack, diversionary bombs, assassination of our President and Vice President and of the Russian President was all written in the notebook." David paused and continued with a heavy strain in his voice, "He did it Mike. He did not want to. He is not like us. But I pressured him Mike. I pressured him and he agreed." Dave paused again and then, taking a deep breath, said, "God forgive me Mike. They killed him. They killed this gentle little man. They killed Henry. He was my friend and I used him. He is dead because of me."

"Dave, what happened?"

"He was on his way to Langley when they hacked into the on-board computers on his car through his car's emergency GPS unit. They had a car behind him close enough to make the connection and forced Henry's car to accelerate to an excessive speed. They electronically disabled his breaks. He was so scared Mike. I heard it all. He called me to tell me what he read in the notebook. He told me he had no control over his car. He begged me to help him. We took out the assailant but it was too late. Henry's car went right into an overpass abutment at over 130 miles per hour. He was on the phone to me all the time. God rest his soul. God forgive me."

"I am sorry Dave. I am so sorry," Michael said and then asked, "Are you going to pick up Harris?"

"No. Not yet. We have nothing but a recording of Henry. We will need more than that to nail this treasonous bastard," David responded. "I called because I wanted you to know about Harris and I also want you to promise me that you will protect yourself. I want you to go straight to FSB headquarters to ride the day out. There is nothing more you could do. The Russians and the Agency have it from here. I wanted to let you know you were right. Let's talk again later over the link," David added. Michael agreed to do as David asked. He encouraged David not to blame himself but knew that David would carry Henry's death with him to his grave.

Halil's call awakened Rushad at the staging site in Reutov. He was sleeping in a make shift bedroom on the first floor of the house, while the three members of the Moscow cell slept on the second floor. Rushad and Halil were both using disposable phones to lessen the chance of their call being intercepted. Halil explained that Speaker Harris had a problem and though Halil had the problem resolved, they should assume that some of their plans were exposed. There was nothing to do other than to be aware and prepared to make adjustments. Rushad thanked him and said his cell would handle any trouble. This being the last communication they would risk prior to the completion of the mission, they wished each other well, praised Allah and ended the call. Rushad thought about the mission for a few minutes and then decided to get a few more hours of sleep.

When Vladimir stormed into the situation room in the Lubyanka Building, Alexander was already there to greet him. The link with Langley was live. John Henderson was on the main screen.

"Good Morning Vlad," John said, "I think we need to narrow the possible stations where these bombs will be placed. From the intelligence gained, we know that there is only one station targeted. We also know that the station will be close enough to where our Presidents are scheduled to be at the time of detonation. The plan is for the explosions to divert attention so that an attack by drones would not be immediately detected. We can assume that the drones swill be small and not capable of carrying enough fire power to penetrate even a modest structure. Hence, we believe the assassination attempts will be made outside," John explained.

John continued, "Our President and our Vice President are scheduled to address a media event in the Rose Garden of the White House at 9:30 a.m. our time. We alerted our Secret Service, but the President will not cancel the event. The Secret Service is confident of protecting our leaders because it is almost impossible to enter White House air space undetected. If we are correct that the assassinations are to be simultaneous, then the attempt on your President will be in Moscow at 6:30 p.m.," John paused and asked, "What is your President's schedule?"

"Our President is scheduled to be on the Kremlin Wall as part of a commemoration event regarding the centuries of history associated with various iterations of the Wall. It is also a media event and is planned for outside," Vladimir answered.

"It does not surprise me that they planned this around media events. Viktor and Andrei wanted to give their Chechen hired hands more reason to go all out. A simultaneous assassination attempt being televised would, even if it all failed, would still send a strong message to the world for their cause. I am sure this is exactly what they are planning."

"I agree. This strategy of throwing the leadership of both countries into chaos and having hand-picked replacements walk right into power is really quite brilliant. I am comfortable that we could stop anything coming from the skies above the Kremlin, so there will be no need for our President to cancel his event. We will put the President's security detail on alert," Vladimir said.

"We need to stop the bombs. The bombs are designed to kill innocent people and more may die from the panic that follows the blast, as well as the release of what we now can confirm will be a deadly gas. They are looking for more panic than death, but death will come if we don't prevent those detonations, which is why they targeted Metro stations at respective rush hours in both cities. For that panic to be effective and momentarily divert some attention at both the White House and the Kremlin, the station they choose will need to be close to those buildings."

"Yes, John. I ordered the organization of several surveillance teams to be dispatched to a number of stations. I also ordered six rapid deployment squads to be positioned strategically in and around the Kremlin. Any and all of these squads will be able to respond within less than two minutes to any of the stations we have identified, and even faster to some of the stations. Our surveillance people know what they are looking for and should be able to call for a squad and have it respond in enough time to stop the bombing," Vladimir explained.

"We think alike, Vlad. We coordinated with our FBI have organized exactly the same defensive structure. We will be ready in Washington."

"John, remember that these people are well connected. They were able to go after your man who read the notebook, they attacked our analyst, Anya and they murdered our agent Petrov, and your agent Moore. They have eyes in place in our cities. Also, they will assume that we are getting close and they will assume that we probably know about some, if not most, of their plans. They will make adjustments, and I don't need to remind you they are most likely ex-military and combat hardened. They will be prepared for a fight."

"I agree. Our rapid deployment squads will be mostly FBI special agents who have been specifically trained for this type of response. I will have CIA field agents with them. Our squads will provide an overwhelming and extremely capable force to successfully control any situation," John said.

"All we need to do now is make sure we see them before they see us," Vladimir said. He and John agreed to keep the link live through the conclusion of whatever comes. This way both organizations will be able to share intelligence in real time. Vladimir and Alexander left the situation room to check on the details of the FSB defense plans. John left the Langley situation room to more closely monitor preparations in Washington.

Anya arrived at The Lubyanka Building at 8:00 a.m., wearing blue jeans, a navy blue sweater, running shoes and a black hooded parka. Her hair was in a ponytail again this morning. She was told to be ready for field surveillance. Her security agents were with her. She met Alexander in his office and was told to assemble with other surveillance personnel in the conference room across the floor. She and twenty other analysts were carefully briefed on the latest intelligence in great detail, divided into ten surveillance pairs and assigned to each of ten Metro stations relatively close to the Kremlin.

The pairs were given photographs of Rushad, Mumadi and the other identified Chechens they were looking for. Each surveillance pair would be accompanied by two heavily armed agents for security and each surveillance analyst would be issued an MP-443 semi-automatic pistol. They were ordered not to approach any of the suspects, but to immediately report positive sightings to Central Control. The nearest rapid deployment squad would then be called in by Central Control. The only time the surveillance pair and its security agents were to take action was if they were attacked, or if they had to intervene to save innocent Russian lives.

Anya was paired with a handsome, athletically built, young man with blond hair and blue eyes named Kirill. Kirill has been in the FSB a year longer than Anya and was known professionally for his fast mind, and personally for his ability to break hearts of young women. Kirill was also dressed casually in jeans, running shoes, a black turtleneck shirt and dark blue ski jacket. Anya's two security agents would stay with Anya and Kirill to provide their protection.

Anya and Kirill were each issued a MP-443 pistol and three fully loaded magazines. They inspected their weapon, pushed one magazine into the handle and, keeping the pistol uncharged as they were ordered, holstered the weapon and put the extra magazines in a coat pocket. The two security agents were issued fully automatic AK-47's and several fully loaded thirty round magazines, in addition to their MP-443 handguns.

Each group of analysts and agents left the Lubyanka Building just before noon and boarded an individual militarized black UAZ Hunter SUV. All the surveillance teams left for their designated posts. Anya's group was assigned to set up across from the main entrance to the Biblioteka Imeni Lenina Station, one of the stations closest to the Kremlin. With one of the security agents driving, the other in the front passenger seat and Anya and Kirill in the back of the vehicle, they parked across the street from the station's entrance and set up their position.

The interior rear of the UAZ was modified to serve as a dual surveillance workstation, equipped with laptop computers and encrypted broad band communications. Cameras were mounted in a concealed fashion around the roof of the SUV. Anya and Kirill, sitting side by side, had full control of all the cameras and could, rise, lower and focus them as they needed. Anya and Kirill each wore a headset and established communications with Central Control. The security agents kept vigil on anything and anyone who came close to the SUV. They were able to view all sides of their position on a small in-dash monitor fed by cameras mounted on the rear hatch and side doors of the SUV. The mobile surveillance unit was completely self-contained and equipped to observe the station, while also monitoring its own perimeter.

"I used the facial recognition software before," Kirill said to Anya. "It works extremely well. We have the images loaded on each laptop and all we have to do is assign a camera image to the scan macro and it will report a match or clear it instantly," he added.

"Thank you. I worked with it in the lab, but this is the first time I am using it in the field," Anya responded.

"You will be impressed with how fast it works," Kirill said. He sat back in his seat and asked, "How are you? I understand that you had a scare the other day."

"I am fine," Anya said in a definite tone. She added, "I appreciate you asking but if that is your way of approaching me, I am not stupid."

"Pleasc, don't believe all that nonsense you may have heard about me with women. I am a good guy. Yes, I like to date but I am always respectful and I never lead women on. I asked about you because you are FSB and I care," he said. He hesitated, smiled and added, "And you are cute."

"Well, Central Control must be enjoying this conversion," Anya, feeling a blush, joked. "Thank you for your concern. I accept it as genuine," she added. The brief exchange was needed to break the ice and the two analysts set about their work in an extremely professional manner. They manipulated the cameras to view various people entering and leaving the station, focusing close up on some and routinely scanning wide angle views, speaking to each other constantly about camera positions. Anya did make a mental note that she was working with quite a handsome man. In the front of the vehicle, the security agents hardly said a word as they kept a close and careful watch on the vehicle's perimeter.

Michael and Ivan arrived at FSB headquarters just after Anya and the other surveillance groups left for their positions. He and Ivan walked into the Alexander's office and were briefed on the actions being taken by both the FSB in Moscow and the CIA in Washington. Alexander told Michael that Vladimir wanted to speak with him. He also said that David Capella was on the link and also wanted to speak with him. Vladimir was in the situation room so everyone was in one place, with David on the link. Alexander invited Ivan to join them and the three men walked into the situation room.

Inside the situation room, Vladimir was speaking to David. "Dave, I am sorry that a brave man lost his life. From what I heard about Mr. Henry Madison he was someone who deserves my respect and admiration," Vladimir said.

"Thank you. Henry was a good man. He was my friend," David responded. Ivan and Alexander added their condolences as they entered the room with Michael.

"Good Morning Dave. Again, I sorry about Henry," Michael said.

"I thank you gentlemen. We have much to do today to prevent the loss of any more innocent lives in both of our countries. Mike, I spoke with John and we appreciate all you have done. It was well beyond your assignment and now the Agency is concerned for your safety. We want you to stand down. I believe you are scheduled to return home this evening?"

"I am supposed to be on an evening flight, but I really don't want to be at 40,000 feet while this is all being sorted out."

"Understood, but stay at FSB headquarters and out of trouble. How will you explain the extra time in Moscow to Bricksen Grove?"

"No worries, I missed flights before. Besides, when all this unfolds, I can guarantee that flights will be delayed and probably canceled," Michael said. David nodded in agreement but again ordered Michael to stand down from this point forward.

Alexander changed the conversation to logistical matters related to surveillance in Moscow and Washington. While Alexander spoke about logistics, Vladimir asked Michael and Ivan to join him outside of the situation room to discuss Enerprov and Andrei.

In the hallway, Vladimir looked Michael in the eye and asked, "You have no intention of standing down, do you?"

"No Sir, none whatsoever."

"Ivan," Vladimir called and said to him, "You stay with our American friend and keep him safe."

"Da," Ivan responded in Russian as he snapped to attention.

"Are you sure, Vladimir?" Michael asked. He added, "I have disobeyed Dave before. He knows me. Let me take the heat, you have been extremely helpful and I don't want to hurt our countries' cooperative action."

"Mr. Clark, Mike. I told you before. You are family now. You are FSB. We are loyal to our own and we will stand with you. You have no say in this. Ivan will stick with you, as you Americans say, like he is glued on you," Vladimir said it a way that offered no room for discussion. Michael thanked him and they began to talk about Enerprov. Vladimir said he would call Pavel and update him on all they know. He assured Michael that if Andrei has Viktor's notebook with him,

Pavel would get his hands on it. Vladimir agreed that the notebook would be important evidence against both Andrei and James Harris and they had to have it.

By 4:00 a.m. in Washington, all of the combined CIA and FBI surveillance groups and rapid deployment squads were positioned throughout the city. Langley was Central Control and all the groups were acting on orders similar to their FSB counterparts. The only difference was that the CIA, together with the FBI, has twelve surveillance groups and eight rapid deployment squads. Everyone was positioned and working.

A few hours later, the Landover cell started to get ready. Halil, Kerim, Elbek and Abbas dressed in black, wearing military style boots, cargo pants, sweaters, heavy waste length jackets and ski caps. Each carried a holstered MP-443 Grach and each had a duffle bag loaded with heavier weapons and ammunition. Before they went any further, they knelt on all fours with their heads to the floor facing east and prayed for several minutes. The group stood up, wished each other well and the mission began.

Elbek and Abbas removed the tarp from Kerim's car and carefully placed the bomb on rear seat and secured it with a seat belt. They put their duffle bags in the trunk and with Abbas in the driver's seat headed off into Washington.

Halil and Kerim carried the Russian ZALA 421-12 drones to the driveway and carefully positioned them for launch. They planned to use the driveway as a runway to launch the drones without notice. All of the control equipment is set up on the rear deck of the house. Halil and Kerim will use the drones' GPS navigation systems to guide them to the targets. The drones will fly well below the elevation that defensive radar will be scanning. By the time the drones are detected they will be in decent and have fired their missiles.

Elbek and Abbas slowed down as they crossed into Washington from Maryland. They were concerned about how well the police and Federal agencies would be prepared for them due to the incident with Speaker Harris' chief-of-staff. To compensate, they left earlier than originally planned so they would have more time to select the most vulnerable Washington Metro station closest to the White House.

They decided to park and wait for traffic to build and for Bashir to be on the road, before they chose the station for the bomb. Additional traffic and the hustle of the business morning will give them more cover when they select the target site. For now, they will wait and observe.

In Reutov, the same routine took place with the Moscow cell. They were also dressed in black and heavily armed. Rushad joined the two cell members assigned to plant the bomb, leaving the fourth man to operate the ZALA. Rushad wanted to be in Moscow in case anything went wrong. He was also still intent on grabbing Anya and using her as either a hostage to insure a safe escape, or as bait to lure the American to his death. They drove to the Reutov-Moscow line, parked and waited for the when Mumadi was scheduled to leave his apartment.

Chapter 24

Pavel, sitting behind his desk in his office at Enerprov, hung up the phone slowly after his conversation with Vladimir. The strategy to assassinate the leadership of both Russia and the United States simultaneously, have predetermined people assume power and form a cooperative union between the two countries, could not possibly be true. He could not believe all that Vladimir told him. But Pavel knew that Vladimir was an honest man and a patriot. Vladimir was like a brother. They served in brutal combat together in Afghanistan in the early 1980's. Vladimir would never lie to him. The strategy must be real. Most people who knew Viktor Chekhov would agree that he had a wild imagination. Those who knew him well understood that everything Viktor dreamed would happen was exactly what he intended to happen. This crazy plot, this strategy, was not any different than the other dreams of the former black market criminal. Viktor once envisioned an energy company growing from nothing into a world leader. Enerprov is proof that Viktor's imagination was never to be regarded as anything other than serious.

Andrei was in his office getting ready to leave the city before 4:00 p.m. Most other Enerprov personnel at the Moscow headquarters left by noon because it became a custom after Viktor's death, to honor the founder's birthday by giving all employees a half day.

The building was empty accept for certain security staff and employees handling important customer or production issues. Pavel called to see if Sasha, Andrei's assistant, was still at her desk. Her auto-response said she had gone for the day. Pavel's second call was to Andrei's direct line.

"This is Andrei," Andrei said.

"Pavel here, Sir. I need to see you. A small emergency," Pavel said.

"I am about to leave the city Pavel. Can it wait till next week when I will be back in the office?"

"Please Andrei. It is important and I promise it will not take long," Pavel assured him.

"Come on up, but plan on being quick. Sasha has left, so just knock and then come directly into my office," Andrei said.

Pavel put the phone down, unlocked the top right drawer of his desk where he kept his MP-443 Grach. He picked up the gun and a loaded magazine and pushed the magazine securely into place in the handgrip. He pulled back the slide and released it, charging the pistol with a round in the chamber. Pavel stood put the gun in his waistband and covered it with his jacket. He left his office and walked to the elevator.

When the elevator stopped at the sixtieth floor and the doors opened, Pavel stepped off and walked into the empty waiting room outside of Andrei's office. He looked at his wristwatch and saw that the time was just 4:00 p.m. He had planned on delaying Andrei's departure to see if he would reveal that he was nervous to leave the city, but there was no need for that now. The objective was the notebook and nothing else. He continued to walk past Sasha's vacant desk and knocked on Andrei's door.

"Pavel, come on in and sit down," Andrei said.

"Thank you for seeing me Sir," Pavel said as he sat down in a chair facing Andrei, who was seated behind his desk. "A happy birthday to Viktor," Pavel added.

"My father always liked you Pavel. I believe you were one of the first employees at Enerprov. Is that correct?' Andrei asked.

"Number nine," Pavel responded. "Viktor needed to hire the geologists first, then security. I liked Viktor as well."

"So, what is this problem that cannot wait a few days?"

Pavel thought that the only way forward at this point was to be blunt. He came right out and said, "The problem Sir is Viktor."

Andrei, who had been shuffling papers in preparation for leaving, stopped what he was doing and leaned back in his chair and looked directly into Pavel's eyes. "Viktor?" he said.

"Your father was a dreamer, but his dreams were more than casual thoughts. You know that better than anyone else that Viktor's dreams were all strategies. In 1978 he met an American at a pub across from Lubyanka Station and he dreamed one of his dreams. This one included the American and like his other dreams, it was a sincere strategy," Pavel said in a slow and deliberate manner.

"What are you talking about? A strategy from 1978? What is this Lubyanka strategy you speak of and where are you getting this nonsense?" Andrei, showing signs of concern, said indignantly.

"Not nonsense, the truth and you know it. Viktor conceived of toppling the leadership of our country and the United States. New leadership would be pre-chosen by Viktor and his American friend. The two countries would then cooperate politically and economically, with Viktor pulling the strings. It turns out that his American friend is now the United States Speaker of the House, Mr. James Harris, and the third in line to the presidency. Viktor planned it well. Simultaneously assassinate the President and the Vice President of the United States and the President of today's Russian Federation. Mr. Harris becomes the President of the United States and a chosen person, someone I assume your father selected, becomes our country's President. Nice and neat."

"Please Pavel; go home, there is no such strategy."

"The notebook. The CIA saw Harris' notebook and I am here to retrieve your father's," Pavel said as clearly as possible.

"What notebook?" Andrei asked.

"The one I am guessing is in your briefcase," Pavel said as he glanced at the small brown leather briefcase that was on the top of Andrei's desk to his left.

"I can handle this two ways Pavel. I can deny everything you are saying and order you from my office. Or," he paused as he reached for the briefcase and continued, "I could show you that there is nothing in my briefcase and then ask for your resignation. You choose. I owe you that much for your years of loyal service to my father. Choose, but please take the first option and let us accept that you are a fool having a foolish moment; you keep your job; and we never speak of this again. If you choose the second option, I will show you that you are fool and you resign. Which is it going to be?" Andrei asked as he put his hand in the briefcase.

Pavel had already removed his MP-443 from his waistband and was holding it in his lap as he sat staring at Andrei. He knew that if the notebook was in the briefcase, Andrei's hand would be on a gun in that briefcase. If the notebook was not in the briefcase, then Pavel would have to either walk away without challenging Andrei or resign in disgrace when proven wrong. Whatever was going to happen in the next few seconds would not have a good outcome for one of them.

"Well, I really want to get on my way. Make a choice Pavel," Andrei demanded.

Pavel, trusting Vladimir's findings and his own instincts, braced for what he was sure would follow and quietly said, "Prove me the fool. Show me what is in the briefcase."

Andrei did not even take a breath. He coldly fired a shot from the Berretta 92-FS in the briefcase, through the briefcase, hitting Pavel in the chest and knocking him backwards in his chair. Andrei stood, pulled the Berretta from the briefcase and aimed it directly at Pavel face. But before he could squeeze the trigger a second time, Pavel fired three successive rounds directly into Andrei's heart. Andrei fell backwards, over his chair and on to the floor dead.

Pavel dropped his gun and stopped the bleeding from his chest by applying pressure with his right hand. He remained sitting for a minute to catch his breath and to be sure that he had his wound under control. He took a deep breath and reached across the desk with his left hand for Andrei's briefcase, and pulled it toward him. Once he had it on his side of the desk, he reached in with his left hand and took out the old notebook. He put it on the desk and opened it. Viktor's notes said it all. He turned to the final entries, to see Andrei's notes reveal that revealed the sad truth about a son who lived his entire life to please a father who could not be pleased. Andrei's entries all concluded with, "Just to please you father."

Pavel turned Andrei's phone around and dialed Vladimir's personal number at the FSB. When Vladimir answered, Pavel wasted few words and said, "I have the notebook. Andrei is dead. I am shot in the chest. Please send help now," Pavel hung up the phone and leaned back in his chair. He took another breath and used the phone a second time. This call was to his own security people. He told them to expect FSB; to call an ambulance; and to come up to Andrei's office immediately.

Bob Bonelli

## Chapter 25

Michael, sitting in Alexander's office, thought about the use of drones for the assassination attempts and could not see how a small group of embedded cell members could possibly pull that off. Any drone capable of carrying sufficient ordnance for the task would be too large to launch undetected. The only conclusion is that a small drone designed for non-lethal operation would have to be modified to carry a small weapon. He asked Alexander if the Russians had such a drone. Alexander had a few analysts do some research and he came back to Michael with his findings.

"The ZALA 421-12," Alexander said. "It is small, electric powered, limited range, but can be modified to carry something deadly and can be launched from a residential driveway," he added.

"Range?" Michael asked

"Maybe forty kilometers, at best, but that would take almost an hour."

"So if you were going to target the Kremlin and you did not want it detected, how long would you risk it being in flight?" Michael asked.

"No more than thirty minutes," Alexander answered.

"What distance can the ZALA cover in thirty minutes?"

"No more than twenty kilometers," Alexander answered, as he brought up a map of Moscow on the computer terminal in his office. He then expanded the map to show areas as far as twenty kilometers from the Kremlin and there it was. "Reutov!" Alexander said. "We keep coming back to Reutov. It has to be where the location of the site," he said.

"Let's get on the link and share this with the CIA and see if they can predict something similar for Washington," Michael suggested.

The CIA analysts had no doubt that the staging area for the Washington attack would be close to the Capitol district and since all the evidence pointed to the cell being located in Landover, it was logical to conclude that the staging area would also be in Landover. When the FSB suggested that the drones would be launched from a distance no more than twelve miles from the city, the radius of possible locations included parts of Virginia and Maryland's southern communities. Landover was at the top of the list. David Capella, on the link said, "I think we go north. The launch has to be planned for someplace in Southern Maryland and Landover is the most likely location."

With issue settled, waiting attack helicopters were deployed in both cities. If they could not find the drones on the ground, the chopper crews had the clearance to destroy them in flight.

"Michael, are you sure you don't want to join the Agency full time?" asked David.

"Nope. I am a happy independent," he said.

Vladimir, who had just taken Pavel's call, walked into the situation room. Before he said anything about Pavel, he asked about why the helicopters were deployed and he was pleased with the analysis. "Thank you again, Mike," he said. "We are going to miss you when you return home," he added.

Vladimir updated everyone on the link, about Andrei, "Our people are on their way to Enerprov. Pavel took one bullet to his chest. He is a tough old bird and he is hard to kill. I am sure he will be fine. He has Viktor's notebook. Unfortunately, Andrei is dead. Pavel said Andrei fired first and was about to finished the job, but Pavel was prepared and settled matters quickly. He had no other choice. Pavel's brief look at the notebook confirms everything. We were right, but the threat is far from neutralized. We have to stop these people from taking innocent lives and we don't have much time."

"I agree Vlad," John Henderson said, walking into the Langley situation room in time to hear the update. "Our people are in motion. We will need a copy of the notebook Vlad," John added.

"You will have it, John," Vladimir assured him.

Bob Bonelli

"Speaker Harris? What is the next step with him?" Michael asked.

"We have eyes on him Michael," David answered and continued with, "He is not going anywhere and we can pick him up as soon as this is all over."

John Henderson interrupted and said, "Vladimir is right. Our major concern now is to save innocent lives. The Secret Service has been warned of a possible airborne attempt on the President and the Vice President. They will be ready at the White House and our choppers should find the drones before they reach the target site."

"Our people at the Kremlin are equally ready and our choppers are also in motion. I think we can be sure that our leaders are safe. Our focus has to be our citizens," Vladimir said.

FSB response units arrived at Enerprov within minutes and squads dressed for combat and armed with automatic AK-47's jumped from several KAMAZ BPM-97 armored vehicles and deployed around the Enerprov Building. They shut off all exits with military efficiency and formed a secure perimeter around the building.

Another squad, equally dressed and armed, entered the Building with three medical specialists and went directly to Andrei's office. Pavel was still bleeding, but the constant pressure he applied slowed the bleeding to a trickle. The medical specialist took over and it was clear that Pavel would be fine. The bullet missed his heart, but only by a hair. Either he was lucky or he had an angel on his shoulder.

Another medical specialist confirmed that Andrei was dead.

Pavel declined to be taken to the hospital until he handed Vladimir the notebook himself. The squad's commander agreed and ordered Pavel to be taken to the Lubyanka Building and then to the hospital. Vladimir was called and said he would meet the transport in front of FSB headquarters.

The time in Moscow reached 4:50 p.m. and Mumadi got ready to leave for the staging site. The instructions on the website were clear. He was to leave at 5:00 p.m. and drive for several miles in the opposite direction from the site in Reutov. When he arrives at a particular location, he will wait at that location until he is contacted on his mobile phone. The plan is for him to act as a decoy, knowing that the FSB was watching him and that they would surely follow him. Mumadi was unarmed.

In Landover at 7:50 a.m., Bashir eagerly got into his car and started the engine. The instructions on the website indicated that his part of the mission was to act as a decoy. He was to drive into Washington, stay in the inner-city area away from the Capitol and downtown business districts and pull into a public parking lot. Once there, he was ordered to wait until his mobile phone rang with further instructions. He was disappointed at not being with the rest of the cell, but happy to be on a real mission for the Chechen people. Bashir was unarmed.

The FSB agents watching Mumadi's apartment saw him enter his vehicle and drive off. They followed him from a safe enough distance so they wouldn't be noticed. They knew he was taking them away from Reutov and they knew the staging site was in Reutov, but Mumadi had to be observed and he was their assignment.

The FBI agents assigned to Bashir's home, watched him enter his vehicle and drive south. They followed him into Washington's inner city. They maintained a safe distance to be clear from Bashir's sight. They followed him off the highway on to a local road.

When Bashir pulled into the parking lot of a strip mall whose only open store was a Dunkin Donuts, the agents drove past the parking lot and turned left across the road into another lot where the only open establishment was a McDonalds. They had a clear view of Bashir who was sitting in his car, reading.

Mumadi turned off the road on which he was driving and into the parking for a group of shops. He turned his engine off and leaned his head back in the seat as if to get ready for a nap. The FSB agents following him drove past and turned across the road into another lot in front of a similar group of shops.

CIA Central Command was notified by the agents assigned to Bashir that he stopped and looked like he was taking up a position.

FSB Central Command received the same notice about Mumadi.

After about thirty minutes of no movement from either Bashir or Mumadi, Alexander figured it out. "Something is not right," Alexander said. "Why are these men waiting in the open? They are decoys and nothing more. Why are they not moving?" he said, and then he realized what was going on. "Alert the crews following Mumadi and Bashir to take cover," Alexander shouted over the link. On the Langley side of the link, David Capella immediately understood exactly what Alexander had just figured out. But, there was no time for either organization to react.

Bashir's mobile phone rang. Mumadi's mobile phone rang. A second later the blasts went off in almost perfect synchronization. Bashir's vehicle jumped more than ten feet straight up in a ball of flames with parts and shrapnel thrown thirty feet in every direction. The car hit the ground with a thud, fully engulfed in flames. Shop windows were blown out, but the early hour had only a few people present. Some did get hit with glass and metal shards, but the injuries were minor.

Mumadi's car blew out sideways in all directions with parts and shrapnel hurled more than sixty meters, and then a second explosion of the vehicle's gas tank engulfed it in flames. Shop windows were blown out and some shoppers were hit with flying debris of glass, metal or both. No serious injuries, but a good deal of fear.

Attention in Moscow was turned toward the explosions long enough for Rushad and his bomb team reached their primary bomb location, Biblioteka Imeni Lenina Station, without being noticed. That changed when Anya and Kirill both picked up positive ID's on their facial recognition system.

Rushad noticed the UAZ Hunter and he immediately adjusted the plan. He told the cell member carrying the bomb in a backpack to go directly into the station and proceed with the detonation. Rushad and the other cell member then reached into their duffel bags, which they dropped on the ground, and pulled out the AK-47's and several RGO hand grenades. They switched the AK's to automatic and started to charge the FSB vehicle, firing a barrage of bullets at the SUV.

Anya screamed to Central Command, "Hostels identified; 100% positive; two attacking our vehicle; shots fired; one hostile on his way into the station with a backpack."

"Copy, squad is on the way. Repeat, squad is on the way. Abort your position immediately. Do not engage hostiles," was the order from Central Command. The FSB agent in the driver's seat started the UAZ's engine while the agent in the passenger seat pulled back the bolt of her AK-47 to fully cock the weapon. Anya and Kirill braced in the back. But before the agent could get her window down to act defensively, Rushad threw one and then another powerful RGO hand grenade at the vehicle. One landed on the hood of the UAZ and other along its side facing the advancing hostels. The explosion on the UAZ's hood shattered the bullet proof glass of the windshield with shrapnel raining in on the agents, who had been killed instantly by the shock wave from the grenade. The second explosion tossed the vehicle over on its side like it was a toy.

Both Anya and Kirill were knocked unconscious by the combination of the blast and ensuing toppling of the vehicle. Rushad sprayed the front seat with bullets, taking no chances that the agents were alive. He pulled open the rear passenger door on the side facing up of the overturned UAZ and saw the defenseless analysts in the back and was about to finish them with his AK-47 when he recognized Anya. He used the AK's strap and slung the rifle around his right shoulder. He then reached inside and pulled the limp Anya out of the vehicle. He removed her MP-443 from the holster and tossed the gun to the ground, lifted her and carried her away while the other cell member took cover behind the overturned UAZ.

Two rapid deployment squads arrived on the scene in KAMAZ BPM-97 vehicles in less than sixty seconds. A squad of ten combat equipped agents, armed with automatic AK-47's, jumped from one vehicle and ran into the station, while another squad of ten equally equipped and armed agents exited the second vehicle and approached the flipped UAZ. The agents approaching the UAZ spread wide to make themselves a difficult target.

The cell member behind the flipped vehicle started firing at the approaching agents in order to give Rushad the time he needed to get way. The FSB squad hit the ground flat on their stomachs, expertly returning a torrent of bullets directly at the cell member while avoiding hitting the vehicle. They knew that there were FSB personnel in the UAZ so they took this precaution to avoid injuring them further. These agents were all marksmen and directed their fire straight at the cell member. The fire fight lasted no more than ten seconds.

Two FSB squad personnel took fire but their injuries were minor. The Chechen cell member did not do as well. He lay dead with his body torn apart by more than forty high velocity 7.62 mm rounds. Rushad was nowhere to be seen and neither was Anya.

In the station, the other squad of ten FSB agents reached the cell member with the bomb. Four of the agents cleared the area of commuters while the other six surrounded the terrorist, four in front of him and two behind him. The Chechen terrorist was kneeling down over the bomb with the quick detonation device on the ground near the bomb and only inches from his reach. All he had to do was throw the switch or fall on it, and the bomb would detonate and send its lethal gas throughout the station. He looked at the agents and he laughed. "Today the Chechen people show the world," he shouted, and then he looked away from the agents and directly at the switch.

The FSB squad was prepared. The two agents behind the cell member ducked to the side, leaving an empty fire zone behind the target. The four agents in front of him aimed their automatic AK-47's square on his chest. The moment the terrorist moved his eyes from the agents to the switch and before he could take a breath, the FSB agents opened fire and put so many rounds into his chest that the force knocked his body straight back and away from the switch. He lay dead, and the station was safe.

It was time to launch the drone, which sat on the concrete driveway along the side of the house in Reutov. The cell member, operating the controls from the back room of the house, watched the drone through a side window. The cell member stay focused on getting the ZALA airborne. He allowed himself a quick smile as he thought about how in thirty minutes he would fire the missile, and how the blast will kill the President and his security detail. They will be outside, completely exposed and thoroughly surprised.

All of sudden his controls started to behave strangely, as if they were being jammed. He saw through the window that the ZALA continued to move slowly but he could not get it to accelerate to launch speed. Suddenly he heard the deafening sound of a MI-28 Havoc attack helicopter. He looked through the large rear window of the house and saw the fearsome beast accelerate toward him. Then, two large rounds fired from the MI-28's 30 mm NPPU-28 cannon and the ZALA, the house and the terrorist were all history.

The same was happening in Washington. The sacrifice of Bashir, though it was across town, still drew enough attention to provide cover for Elbek and Abbas to reach a Metro Station close to the White House. Elbek has taken an AK-47 from the duffle bag, charged the weapon and held it at ready position. Abbas was carrying the bomb in a back pack and they thought for sure that their way to the target would be clear. They ran down the street leading to the station entrance and turned the corner expecting to see a clear path in front of them. But when they turned that corner, they saw more than twenty CIA and FBI agents with M-4's switched to fully automatic, standing between them and the station entrance.

Both men were stunned, but before Abbas could say or do anything, Elbek aimed his AK-47 at the agents, screamed, "Allāhu Akbar!" and opened fire. The return fire from the combined CIA and FBI squad did not stop until both Elbek and Abbas were lying in deep pools of their own blood. The bomb was never armed and the station was safe.

Halil and Kerim, working the controls on the rear deck of the small house, were still not discovered by the three Apache AH-64 attack helicopters that were airborne and searching for low flying ZALA aircraft as well as possible launch sites. The drones' were on the driveway and started to roll forward and accelerate. The one piloted by Halil took off, followed closely by the other one piloted by Kerim. Neither Halil nor Kerim had any idea of how badly the mission was going. They were completely focused on their own work of piloting the drones to the target area and securing both kills.

The ZALA's reached altitude and headed directly on course toward the White House. While this achievement seemed to Halil and Kerim to be victory in motion, all it did was make the drones visible to the Apache AH-64's. Both drones were in air the air for less than two minutes when one of AH-64's locked on both of them. The Apache pilot fired two Hellfire II Missiles and within a few seconds each drone and its missile was completely disintegrated in the sky. What debris that was left would injure no one on the ground.

Halil and Kerim saw their control monitors go blank and all GPS contact with the ZALA's was lost. They were confused and tried everything to bring the controls back to life, then stopped when the ground, the deck and the entire house shook as the two other Apache AH-64's, having traced the GPS signal controlling the drones, were hovering over the empty field behind the Landover site. The choppers dropped to just above the ground, in direct line with the house and facing the deck.

Halil and Kerim picked up their AK-47's and managed to fire a few rounds at the helicopters, but the pilots immediately returned fire with the AH-64's Hydra 70 rocket pods. The house was left in rubble with both Halil and Kerim dead.

The threats to Moscow and Washington were neutralized.

## Chapter 26

Rushad, dressed in military style clothing and under the cover of all the excitement and confusion in the streets, managed to carry the unconscious Anya without raising suspicion. He appeared to be a first responder helping an innocent victim to find safety from the violence. He carried her for several blocks to the hideout he arranged near the targeted station in Moscow. The three story Soviet era apartment building's entrance was down a narrow secluded side street. He unlocked the front door and carried Anya up the steep staircase to the tiny apartment. He unlocked the apartment door and went inside.

He placed Anya on the floor near the back wall of the room he entered. He handcuffed her hands behind her and placed a strip of duct tape across her mouth. Her face was bruised and her jacket was torn, but she was otherwise okay. She slowly came to consciousness and her mind began to race when she realized she was restrained. Her vision cleared and she saw Rushad.

"Miss Petrova," Rushad said. "I am Rushad Umarov. I am a free Chechen. You do as I say and you will not be hurt. You mess with me, you will die. It is that simple. I am in no mood for anything other than complete cooperation. If you understand, just nod your head."

Anya nodded that she understood and watched intently as Rushad went about assembling an array of weapons, cash and three untraceable mobile phones into a backpack. She watched and listened when he entered a number into one of the phones.

He called Andrei's mobile number four times. All four attempts went to voice mail. He then called Halil, and again the call went to voice mail. He tried all of the prearranged numbers and all of them went unanswered. Something, everything must have gone wrong. He threw the phone across the room against the wall smashing it into pieces, which caused Anya to flinch. Rushad then paced back and forth for several minutes, mumbling to himself. He picked up a second phone and entered a number.

This time, his call was answered on the second ring. It was the FSB. He identified himself as the mastermind behind the day's violence and said he has an FSB agent hostage. He was immediately put through to Vladimir.

"My name is Vladimir and I am in charge. To whom am I speaking?" he asked.

"Does it really matter to you? Does it?" Rushad said angrily.

"It does. It does. We can work this out as two men," Vladimir assured him.

"I am Rushad, Rushad Umarov. I am a free Chechen and I have your Anya Petrova. I want safe passage home and I also want the American. I will exchange Anya for him. I want the American in exchange for Anya." he demanded.

"I understand and I will not play with you. I know the American of whom you speak, but I do not have the authority to grant that part of your request. I promise you safe passage to Chechnya and I will keep my word. You know yourself that once you are back in your country no government, the FSB nor the American CIA will be able to touch you," Vladimir pleaded.

"If you do not give me the American, Anya dies tonight. It is that simple," Rushad said. His speech was calm and cold.

"Will you give me five minutes?" Vladimir suggested.

"Fine, I will call again but that is all the time you will have to make your decision," he said and abruptly ended the call. He put that phone down and picked up the third phone to call back.

Vladimir briefed Michael on the situation. Michael said he would have no problem with the exchange. "Does Anya know that this is the man who killed her father?" Michael asked Vladimir.

"I am not sure, but I do know that he will certainly kill you. He wants blood. By now he must suspect, if he does not know, that everything failed. He will not go home a failure. Killing you will be a small victory because he most likely blames you for the failure of the mission. Once he kills you, he will certainly kill Anya. After that, I am sure that he would care less about what happens. He will either take his own life or force us to do it for him. He will not surrender. I cannot let you do this. There has to be another way."

"Vlad, we both know that there is no other way. Let's insist that we will only make the trade if we can see Anya alive at the site of the trade. I will take it from there," Michael assured him and there was no hesitation or doubt in Michaels's voice.

"I have no other answer either, my brother."

The call came in again, as it did before, it was Rushad. "So, do we have a deal?" he said to Vladimir.

"We do, but we want assurance that our analyst will be safe. The American will hand himself over to you, but only if Anya is seen alive at the trade site, which we suggest FSB headquarters, the Lubyanka Building. You leave her with us, and the American will go with you. I guarantee you will have safe passage to Chechnya. When you arrive home, we will expect the American's release," Vladimir said.

Rushad laughed so uncontrollably that he frightened Anya. "Just that simple, do you think I am a fool, or just stupid?"

"I think neither. What do you suggest?"

"Have the American go to the main hall of Lubyanka Station. Have him there at 9:30 p.m. I will come with Anya and she will be alive. We will make the exchange there and at that time," Rushad said and ended the call.

Vladimir looked concerned. He knew that Rushad had other plans. He looked at Michael and said, "She will surely have a bomb strapped to her and he will be holding a dead-man switch in one hand and either a knife or gun in the other. I am sure of that. It is what these people do. I've seen it before. If you reach to grab the switch, he will kill you with the weapon in his other hand. If you kill him, the bomb will take you all."

"I understand," Michael said. "I know what to do and I am ready. We will have only one chance to get it right and it is all up to me. Keep all your people back but ready to support my actions. Please trust me," Michael said.

Rushad looked at Anya and explained that he was not really a bad person. He tried to convince her that he was a patriot. He did not expect her to understand and did not care if she did or not. He just wanted her to know that his motivation was his country and his God. "It is not about you or about me," Rushad told her. "They killed my family! They killed so many Chechen people and the world did not care," he added. Anya, unable to speak because of the duct tape, just stared at Rushad. She heard what he said and felt his emotion. She tried to understand his feeling, but she was doing all she could to deal with her own fear.

Rushad expertly removed the bomb vest from a box he had stored in the apartment. The vest contained enough explosive to kill the person wearing it and anyone within ten feet of that person. He fitted it with a receiver connected to a detonator. He then connected a transmitter to a switch on a plunger, which he would hold in his hand with his thumb over the plunger. If his thumb lifts from the plunger for any reason, the bomb will detonate.

Rushad had no intention of leaving Lubyanka Station alive. His plan was to make the American sweat and then kill Anya, the American and himself by doing little more than letting go of the plunger. If the American grabbed his hand, he would kill the American with the gun in his other hand and then detonate the bomb. Tonight, he would get his revenge. Tonight, he would achieve honor for Chechnya.

Anya was numb as Rushad strapped the bomb vest around her. She had no idea what to expect and her mind was racing. She calmed herself down, prayed to Christ and felt comfort in the fact that Michael, the prince to whom the carved horse on the box belonged, would be there to protect her.

At FSB headquarters, Ivan walked up to Michael and said, "Mr. Clark, I want to help."

"I appreciate that Ivan, but I need to do this alone. If Rushad gets nervous or suspects a trap, he will kill Anya. If Vladimir is right and Rushad does use a bomb, I will only have seconds to interrupt his plans. This is something that only one man can fix, and he wants me." Michael then removed his holstered Glock and handed it to Ivan. "I won't need this. It will only weigh me down. Please keep it and return it to me when this is over," he said.

"I will," Ivan said.

"You are confident, my brother. Are you sure this will work?" Vladimir interrupted.

"It is in God's hands," Michael answered. Vladimir handed Michael a Kevlar vest and said, "Please wear this. It will make me feel better. Michael smiled, took the vest and put it on.

Michael, Ivan and Vladimir left the building and got into a waiting UAZ Hunter, whose driver had the engine running and drove off as soon as the men were in the SUV. Behind them, squads of heavily armed agents and bomb specialists followed in several KAMAZ BPM-97 vehicles. With sirens blaring, the caravan sped its way to Lubyanka Station and got there in seconds.

By the time the FSB caravan arrived at Lubyanka Station, Moscow Police had already cleared the station's entrance and its main hall. The police also evacuated other parts of the station and stopped all train traffic. The station was completely deserted.

Vladimir, Ivan and the FSB agents and specialists took up a position in the rear of the station's main hall, its stoic tile walls brightly lighted and saying more about man's achievements than his lust for greed, power and vengeance. Slowly walking forward from the others toward the center of the hall emerged the lone American. A husband, a father, a soldier, and yes - a prince - Michael Clark confidently and deliberately walked forward. He was wearing only slacks, a long sleeve shirt, dress shoes and the Kevlar vest. In his right hand, down by his side and close to his leg, he held the black, sleek Fairbairn-Sykes fighting knife. The knife's dagger style eight inch blade was made of hardened steel with a surgically sharp edge. Michael was hoping that Rushad's lust for revenge would cloud his judgment and he would not notice the knife. If he did, then things would just have to move faster than planned. Michael stopped midway across the hall and stood there waiting as the station's main clock stuck 9:30 p.m.

On the other end of the station, two figures started walking closer to Michael. One was Rushad and the other, walking just ahead of him, was Anya. Her arms were free and hanging listless from her shoulders. She looked stunned, frightened and completely vulnerable. Anya's face, bruised from the attack on her vehicle, was pale. Her petite body was completely consumed by the dreadful bomb vest wrapped around her. She was helpless.

Michael began to walk toward Rushad and Anya, and they toward him. As they approached each other, Michael quickly closed the gap to less than two feet between himself and Rushad. Anya was standing to the right of Rushad.

Rushad held up his left hand and in it was the dead-man switch, his thumb securely holding down the spring loaded plunger. In Rushad's other hand was an MP-443. Anya looked terrified but at least her mouth was free of the duct tape. As Michael had hoped, Rushad's eyes were focused directly on Michael and were filled with rage. Rushad did not notice the knife.

"Hello American, we finally get to meet each other," Rushad said. "I am Rushad Umarov, a free Chechen. And who are you? Introduce yourself so that we can be friends."

'Mike Clark," Michael answered. "Anya, are you okay?" Michael asked.

"I am," she said, clearly frightened.

"It will all be over soon sweetheart, I promise," Michael said.

"Oh how touching Mr. Mike Clark! You are breaking my heart," Rushad said. "Let me tell you about real tragedy. Let me tell you about the Chechen people," he said as he started to make a speech.

Michael knew this was his only chance. Rushad needed to make this speech, which would end with him detonating the bomb. Michael did not hesitate. In one continuous movement he tightened his grip on the razor sharp commando knife and lunged forward with the knife, blade edge up and rising, slicing off Rushad's left hand precisely where it is joined to the wrist. Michael grabbed the severed hand and transmitter, holding the hand firmly on the plunger with his left hand while he simultaneously turned his body and brought the knife back down and directly into Rushad's heart. He killed him instantly.

Michael, falling to the ground on top of Rushad as he let go of the knife now planted in Rushad's chest, closed both hands around Rushad's severed hand on the plunger. He lay there quietly, covered in Rushad's blood, starring at the severed hand on the plunger.

Anya, frozen with fear, stood perfectly still watching all that transpired when the three FSB bomb specialists, wearing bomb protection suits and wheeling a portable containment vessel, ran up to her and carefully removed the vest from her and placed it into the containment vessel. Two bomb specialists quickly rolled the containment vessel out of the station, running past Vladimir who was now standing by Anya with his arms around her. The third specialist knelt down next to

Michael and carefully cupped his hands over Michael's vice-like grip on Rushad's severed hand. He slowly slid his own thumb over Rushad's thumb on the plunger, allowing Michael to let go. The bomb specialist stood up and walked out of the station holding the severed hand on the plunger. The bomb vest and the plunger will be deactivated safely at another location.

Ivan had run up to Michael, knelt down and put his hand on his friend's left shoulder, He looked Michael squarely in the eyes and said, "Unbelievable!"

Anya, barely able to fully adsorb what she just witnessed struggled to catch her breath. Vladimir, in all his years in the military and with the FSB had never seen anything like it. He let go of Anya and knelt down next to Michael and Ivan. He looked at his American friend and then pulled him into a smothering hug. He released the hug, helping Michael up and said "Thank you again my brother."

Anya, finally able to breath freely and supported by other agents around her, walked over to Michael. She threw her arms around him and he put his arms around her and they embraced while she cried profusely. They stayed that way for minutes and then she pulled back and asked, "Was he the man who killed my father?"

"Yes," Michael answered and they embraced again. "It's over sweetheart, it's all over," Michael assured her.

Bob Bonelli

Chapter 27

Speaker Harris left his home on Monday morning feeling some remorse for Henry and a little concern for Denise's safety, but he thought more about what he would gain from the success of the strategy he and Viktor planned so many years ago. He arrived at his office at 8:30 a.m. and assembled his staff for a moment of silence in honor of Henry. He then went about his schedule for the day.

By 9:30 a.m. the news media was broadcasting reports about explosions in and around Washington and about gunfire in the streets. Several news outlets were reporting anti-terror activity in Landover Maryland. Reports also started coming in about similar events in Moscow. It was becoming clear that all the attacks were defeated. There was no mention of an assassination attempt, not in Washington and not in Moscow. James began to fear the worst. It all failed. "Okay, no problem," he thought to himself. "No one had any reason to suspect him. He would call Andrei later and they would plan the next move. That simple, nothing to be concerned about," he thought to himself.

"Mr. Speaker," one of his young staffers, a pretty woman who had recently graduated from college, approached him and continued, "Your 10:00 a.m. with the Majority Whip. You need to be in the Chamber, Sir."

"Thank you, I will head over," he answered. "See," he thought to himself, "No problem, just a normal day. I will need to have my staff prepare some comments relative to the news, but I will have them handle that after I meet the Majority Whip," he further assured himself.

Speaker Harris put on his suit jacket and started to leave his office to go over to the Chamber via the Congressional subway when he walked into the outer office of the suite and directly into David Capella, who was accompanied by six FBI agents. "Agent Capella," the Speaker said, "May I help you?" he asked.

"Yeah, you God damn treasonous piece of shit, you certainly can," David said, as he pointed to an arrest warrant held by one of the FBI agents. He then waved a printout of Viktor's notebook. "Guess what all the Russian on these pages translates into, Mr. Speaker. I will tell you. It translates into you spending the rest of your life in prison. Oh, that is if you escape the death penalty, you damn bastard!" David said. "Come with us," one of the FBI agents said, as the Speaker was surrounded by the other agents, handcuffed and lead away.

The next morning in Moscow, Ivan arrived at the Kebur Palace Hotel to take Michael to the airport for his flight home. Funny thing about the flights last night, they were all delayed until this morning due to the failed terrorist attacks. Michael was wearing his blue suit, without a tie, and carrying his coat.

Ivan took his luggage, one check-in, one carry-on and a briefcase and loaded them into the SUV. He told Michael he would wait for him outside, because Michael had visitors.

Walking into the hotel, wearing a dark blue dress, tailored red jacket and heels, and carrying her coat, was Anya. She had a good looking young, blond haired, blue eyed man with her. He was wearing a business suit, with a tie, and one arm in a sling which was a result of yesterday's attack. They walked up to Michael and Anya said, "This is Kirill."

Kirill extended his hand to Michael who accepted the polite handshake. "Kirill, this is Michael Clark, my American father," Anya said without hesitation, setting Michael back on his heels, just a bit.

"I guess I should ask your intentions, young man?" Michael mused to Kirill.

"My intentions are pure, Sir. I promise. Right now Anya and I are friends. We'll take it slow from here," Kirill assured Michael, who smiled back.

Anya then pulled Michael away from Kirill and walked with him across the lobby. "I love you Michael. Is that okay? Is it okay for me to think of you as my American father?" She asked, with a shy innocent smile.

"Well, I don't know about this Kirill character. Is he good enough for my Russian daughter?" He said and they both laughed.

She kissed Michael on each cheek and he returned the gesture. They hugged each other tightly, looked into each other's eyes, smiled and walked back to Kirill. Michael said to Kirill, "You be patient with her and always treat her with respect," He looked at Anya and said, "Good bye sweetheart. I will look forward to hearing about what is going on with you and seeing you again soon. I love you." Anya felt tears beginning to form in her eyes, as she watched Michael joined Ivan in the SUV and drive away from the hotel.

A long flight later and another trip through an airport, then a taxi into Midtown Manhattan, Michael Clark found himself in New York at Bricksen Grove, standing at the entrance to his office, drinking an everyman's coffee. Peter Jenkins came by and asked, "My God Michael, did you hear all that happened at Enerprov?" he asked. "Andrei Chekhov is dead. The transaction is on hold. It is terrible and apparently connected to the attempted terrorist attacks yesterday in both Moscow and Washington. What did you hear in Moscow? Did you hear the Speaker of the House was arrested?"

"Peter, all I know is my hotel was kind enough to inform me that the airport was closed and I was welcome to stay the night, compliments of Enerprov. I am sorry about Andrei. I know you and he were friends. I enjoyed meeting him. I did read about Speaker Harris on the way from the airport. Who knew?"

"By the way, Pavel Invanov, Enerprov Head of Security, called and said he was really impressed with you. He also asked me to tell you that his accident was no big deal and he is fine. He said you would know what he means?" Peter said

"Yes. A little inside joke with a new friend," Michael answered.

"Oh, Pavel also said something about someone named Vladimir is keeping an eye on a certain young couple. What the hell did you do over there?' Peter asked.

Michael smiled and said, "I made a few new friends."

Peter thanked him for another good job, welcomed him back and left for the elevator. Michael walked into his office, switched the lights on and dropped his luggage in the corner. He walked around his desk and sat down in his chair and picked up the framed picture of Sharon and Cindy he kept on his desk. They are with God. He accepts that, though his grief is still heavy. He took out his mobile phone, touched the screen to bring up the camera and touched the screen again to display the stored images. He scrolled to the photograph he took of Anya before he left. His heart perked up a little as he looked at her precious face and he thought about his other daughter, only 4,700 miles away.

The End

Made in the USA
Charleston, SC
19 September 2013